The Cursed Apps

A Hardboiled Magic Adventure

TW Allen

Indignant Media

This story was brought to you in part through the sponsorship of:

- Ian Chung

- Nicholas Cosenza

- Tariq Zawahir

For more information on the Hardboiled Magic series, please visit:
https://www.magicdetective.com/

To subscribe to Todd Allen's newsletter (and get a free short story):
https://www.magicdetective.com/newsletter/

Books in the Hardboiled Magic series:

- *Student Loans Paid In Blood*

- *The Cursed Apps*

For John Foster, the warlock who died twice.

Contents

Sh*t Necromancers Say

1. Family Advice

"**Y**our uncle is here to see you," came the voice from the intercom.

"Which uncle?" the Interim CEO said back into the mic.

He waited and there was no reply. Puzzled, he got up and opened his office door. The administrative assistant intercepted him before he could clear the doorframe.

"I think your uncle might be sick," hissed the assistant. "His color is awful."

In the middle of the outer room, the uncle stood, rocking side to side ever so slightly, as though it was hard for him to keep his balance. His color was indeed awful.

"Now your color's draining, too," said the assistant. "Are you sick? Is there something going around?"

The Interim CEO said nothing. His jaw went slack, and his breathing became labored and audible.

"Do I need to call a doctor or something?" asked the assistant.

The uncle walked forward with tentative, unsteady steps. The Interim CEO retreated into his office, his backpedaling equally unsteady. He tried to shut the door, but the assistant was in the way.

"Is there something I need to know?" asked the assistant.

"My uncle died last week," whispered The Interim CEO.

"Then we have your attention," rasped his uncle.

The Interim CEO did not reply.

His uncle stared at him. A blank look turned into a frown. His uncle grabbed the nearest desk by the corner and flipped it, sending papers and computer peripherals flying across the room.

"Now, do we have your attention?" rasped his uncle.

The Interim CEO nodded his head.

"You know what you did," continued his uncle. "You will cleanse the text."

"You need to leave," the assistant took up a defensive position in between the Interim CEO and his uncle.

The uncle took another step closer, brought up an arm, and in a sweeping motion tossed the assistant across the room.

"Do you understand your task?" the uncle's empty eyes were now level with the Interim CEO's.

"Not really," whispered the Interim CEO.

"The text was not meant for the masses," the uncle spoke louder. "You will remove it before you cause even greater harm. It will be removed, or we shall come again, and you will become such as this vessel."

As he stopped speaking, the uncle collapsed onto the floor.

"Is he dead?" asked the assistant, scrambling to stand up.

"He's dead," said The Interim CEO. "He was dead last week. He's dead now. Don't ask me to explain the last five minutes."

2. Explaining the Last Five Minutes

"**A**nd this is where he collapsed?" asked the man in the black suit.

"Right there," the Interim CEO pointed at the floor. "The paramedics said he was dead, but we already knew that. I mean, he'd been embalmed."

"Cremation might be prudent," offered the man in the black suit. "If you have any say in the matter, that is. It's harder for ashes to move around and they tend not to be able to grip and throw things."

"Can you explain what happened here?" asked the Interim CEO. "Does it really boil down to a physics problem?"

"That's why your investor retained me." Mister Lewis had a business card that read "Physics Consultant," but that was something of an in-joke. Mister Lewis consulted on matters that defied the laws of physics. Things that sometimes went bump in the night and weren't spoken of in polite company. "There are a few possible explanations, so I'll need to get some more information from you, and we'll see about eliminating some possibilities."

"Anything you need. This whole ordeal has been very... unsettling. I need an explanation. Closure. And I think I need a drink, too. Would you like anything? One of the perks of the startup world is getting to stock a full bar."

The Interim CEO gestured to a three-tiered shelf of bottles along the office's wall.

"Not at this moment," began Mister Lewis. "Is that a black light under the bottles?"

"Yes, it's a black light LED shelf. It's good for projecting an avant-garde image to investors. Makes us look creative." The Interim CEO poured himself 4 fingers of bourbon and forced down a slug of it.

"Your uncle's body left the cemetery earlier in the day," Mister Lewis returned to the matter at hand. "Looks like he dug his way to the surface and walked over here."

"Walked? I wouldn't call it walking. Staggering maybe."

"Fine. The body staggered over here if that's how you prefer to interpret it. That part's all fairly standard for a reanimation. Zombie. Possession. Whatever you want to call it. All of those conditions have the body leaving the grave. What's a little more unusual is that the departed spoke to you."

"Oh, it spoke all right," the Interim CEO threw back the rest of the bourbon and swallowed hard. "Whatever was speaking wasn't my uncle, though. My uncle never referred to himself with a royal 'we' before. Do the... does a man's personality change after death? Is that what's unusual? More unusual than a dead man visiting my office?"

"That almost certainly wasn't your uncle speaking. And yes, that's the unusual part. Zombies happen, those aren't all that unusual in the greater scheme of things. A reanimated body speaking to you is a little more unusual. A reanimated body speaking with someone else's voice and making demands? That suggests control by the living, and that's not exactly a beginner's trick. It also doesn't mean this threat was originated by someone steeped in the black arts. I'm not the only person who... consults... and it could have been conducted on someone's behalf. The real question is who could you have pissed off badly enough to send something as personal as a deceased family member to deliver the message?"

"I don't know. I don't think I've even been here long enough to make any enemies."

"Explain that."

"I'm new to the job," The Interim CEO fished a cigar out of his desk. He paused to fumble with a triple jet torch lighter and almost lit the cigar in the middle before getting a grip on himself. "I mean, my family's from here, but I haven't really spent any time on this side of the country in 10 years. I was hired to try and salvage this startup and I've only been back a couple weeks."

"Fine. Let's start with the salvaging. What exactly does this place do and what happened to make you need to fix it?"

"We're an online slang dictionary. People use us to find out what the new slang means. Or the old slang. The site's slang records go back quite a long time. I suppose it's easiest to say I'm here because of performance issues."

"And by that you mean?"

"Startups can be judged a few different ways. How many different people use an app. How quickly the number of users is growing. If the users aren't growing, sometimes investors start caring about how much money the app is making. That's the short version. The app wasn't growing very fast, and it wasn't generating much revenue, so I stepped in to facilitate more user growth. It was intimated that my predecessor was spending too much time pursuing niche markets that were too small to move the needle. At some point they'll replace me with someone more permanent. I'm here to get things restarted."

"OK, so you're here to get more traffic. What happened to the old CEO?"

"Technically, I replaced The Founder of the company."

"Did The Founder leave amicably?"

"Does that ever happen?" the Interim CEO took a long drag off his cigar. "Founders tend to be a little paternal about it. The startup is their child. Their life. Frequently, their sense of self-worth is tied up in the company. They almost always have a fit when their company outgrows them and it's time for someone with more experience in running a company to take over. It's usually worse if they weren't preforming to expectations and someone has to be brought in to salvage the startup. It's bad for the ego, but salvaging startups is what I do for a living. This time, The Founder wasn't actually around by the time I arrived, so I can't speak to mental state. Either The Founder has simply moved on or The Founder is too mad to talk to me. Nothing's out of the ordinary with either of those options."

"So, we can't actually rule The Founder out as an instigator at this time. I can look into that later. Right now, let's focus on the demand that was made. Do you have any idea what this 'text' is that they want cleansed?"

"The entire app is a text. I mean, some cranks complain about the dirty parts. But then again, people complain to the lyrics apps about profanity in hip hop. You find what you look for."

"That might be too literal. Let's see if there's a connection to... the way the message was delivered. Let's look a few things up."

"I can do that," said the Interim CEO as he produced an oversized smartphone from his pocket. "Fire away."

"What happens if you type in zombie?"

The app read: Zombie – One who follows without question.

"All right, how about ghoul?"

The app read: Ghoul – One who devours political news.

"So, your app is like Bierce's Devil's Dictionary. Fine. Let's go further abroad. How about reanimation?"

"I..." began the Interim CEO. "Are these instructions?"

He held up the phone, and the app displayed a numbered list.

"That's real," whispered Mister Lewis. "And yes, those are instructions. Modernized instructions. The original text isn't numbered. What happens if you type in goety?"

"I've never heard," began the Interim CEO.

"You wouldn't have," Mister Lewis interjected. "Think of it as technical jargon for wizards and witches. It involves invocations. Let's see how deep this goes. G-O-E-T-Y."

Again, the app displayed a list of instructions.

"That reanimated body may have had a point," Mister Lewis paused to exhale. "This really is dangerous. Those are working instructions for two rituals and if those rituals aren't performed correctly... do you have records of who put that in your system?"

"It's a crowdsourced app," began the Interim CEO, "You can't enter anything into it without the user being tagged. I already know that login, too. The Founder put those in."

"And if it was no longer desirable to have those online, wouldn't The Founder be able to delete them or is that something the company has to do?"

"Users have the ability to delete their entries. Delete their whole accounts if they want to. It would just be a matter of logging in and clicking a few buttons."

"Then it's not an accident those are still up. What other 'definitions' did The Founder add to that app? Can you show me the user record?"

"One moment," the Interim CEO fiddled with his phone. "Resurrection. Divination. Binding. What does 'theurgy' mean?"

"It's similar to a binding, but you really don't want to know the details. Look, could..." Mister Lewis was interrupted by a crashing sound from the outer office.

As Lewis and the Interim CEO peered out the office door, they discovered they had a visitor. A visibly decayed body was overturning furniture and moaning.

"I think I will have that drink," said Mister Lewis. "151. Give me the whole bottle. And your lighter."

"151 is a little down market to convey prestige. We have an Appleton 21. It's very nice."

"I need something stronger. Chartreuse. Green Chartreuse. Is that up market enough?"

"Of course," he said, backing up to the bar. He handed over a bottle of Green Chartreuse without further comment.

"And the lighter?"

Mister Lewis took the Chartreuse and the lighter and stomped over to where the decomposing body was trashing the outer office. He held the bottle aloft with his right hand and brought it down hard onto the dead thing's clavicle, breaking the bottle and showering its shoulder and chest with herbal liqueur. In his left hand, he ignited the lighter, turned up the length of the jet and jabbed at the thing's chest until the Chartreuse ignited. Then he kicked a leg out from under it.

The still-moving body fell over. The remains of the clothing it wore were combusting.

"Fire's good for cleansing, isn't it?" Mister Lewis spoke to the body, hoping its masters were listening. Then he grabbed a notebook off a nearby desk and dropped it on the body. The notebook started to smolder.

"You," Mister Lewis pointed at the administrative assistant. "I need a couple reams of paper. Quickly."

They were brought, though perhaps not quickly enough. Lewis ripped one open and started dropping them in small batches, using it as kindling to build the fire and occasionally kicking the body as it attempted to rise.

"I think that was my cousin," stammered the assistant.

"Whoever's behind this is doing their homework," replied Mister Lewis. "Incidentally, what's wrong with your sprinkler system? Usually, offices get a little wet when you start a bonfire."

"I don't think the sprinklers came online after the building was retrofitted," offered the Interim CEO. "I suspect our Investor would refer to it as a cost control."

"That sounds about right," Mister Lewis rolled his eyes. "This is not my first contract with your Investor."

"Can I have my lighter back?"

"Fine," Mister Lewis dropped another fistful of paper onto the burning body and then returned the lighter. "Here's how we're going to play this. I'm going to keep this fire going until this thing stops moving. We're going to burn the reanimation right out of it. Then I'm going to go find this Founder of yours and ask what's being played at with those necromantic 'slang' instructions. While I'm doing that, you're going to go through that app and delete everything The Founder uploaded that remotely resembles anything like what we just looked at. Anything that looks like sorcery or involves the dead. Get it off the servers. Torch the backups."

"I don't think our policy allows," began the Interim CEO.

"Then make a new policy," snapped Mister Lewis. "You know why I'm here and who sent me. Just assume my words come from above. You're incurring liability having that information online. This thing I'm burning is the latest incident of corporeal liability showing up to do you harm. It's not clear to me if you can also incur legal liability from this, but your Investor does not like liability of any kind. Are you following me?"

"I can have everything removed from the servers."

"Good. Additionally, it might be a good idea to barricade the door after I leave. If The Founder isn't the one who sent this delightful messenger, I can't guarantee you won't have another visitor before I can sort this out."

3. The Loneliness of the Long-Distance Founder

It wasn't an impressive house as such things went, but the neighborhood made it expensive enough. Two stories with a stoop and a narrow frame. A paint job that needed some touching up. In the back was a small yard with overgrowth that could've been a garden, had someone bothered. It was in that yard, Mister Lewis found his wayward Founder playing with a dead frog.

"Rise and be whole," exclaimed the Founder with all due gusto.

The frog didn't move, just like dead things usually don't.

The Founder stared pensively for a moment, then produced a piece of chalk and drew a circle around the frog.

"The breath of life greets and lifts you," shouted The Founder, arms waving in the air.

The frog still wasn't moving.

"I don't think you're following the directions right," Mister Lewis spoke softly and watched The Founder jump. "You're drawing a circle with chalk instead of salt. The chalk is for the runes outside the circle. You skipped that part entirely. Most importantly, you don't yell the breath of life into it, you pucker up and blow it in. Like CPR."

The Founder frowned for a moment, then picked up the frog, puckered up and blew air into the frog's mouth. The Founder almost dropped the frog in the process, yet the frog still did not stir.

"OK, I confess," chuckled Mister Lewis. "I made up the bit about the breath of life. You really are new at this, aren't you?"

"Who the hell are you and why are you in my back-yard?" The Founder's cheeks were flush, but the hiss was much quieter than the attempts at incantations.

"I'm here to try and clean up your mess," beamed Mister Lewis, laying it on a bit too thick. "We need to have a chat about what you were trying to do just now and what you left on the servers at your startup."

"My former startup," barked The Founder, redder still, throwing the frog to the ground. "The Investor made it perfectly clear I have nothing to do with that anymore. I never should've taken venture capital. I was diluted right out of ownership and shown the door."

"Let's take it down a notch. There's a real problem with what you put on that server and if you don't fully understand what you were starting with that, then you don't understand you've broken the rules and the powers that be are coming for you. These are heavy hitters and if they come in force, there's only so much I can do about it. You clearly don't have any experience with necromancy, so what are you doing fooling around with it and why were you posting rituals on a website?"

"It's not a website," growled The Founder. "It's an app that happens to have a website."

"Let's not get any more pedantic or I'll forget I'm trying to help you here," groaned Mister Lewis. "You seem a little young to be caught up in this. How old are you, anyway?"

"20."

"And you were apprenticed to a necromancer when you were let go?"

"No, I was running my startup for the last year and a half," The Founder's eyes rolled like a boss. "You know how it works. Drop out of college, start a company, sell the company in 18 months? Instead of the company selling, I got sold out."

"What, just a pure tech play? I don't see where the occult factors into this."

"It's a demographic," The Founder paused to step on an ant that had crawled up out of the grass. "The app user base stopped growing. We plateaued. I was under a lot of pressure to grow the number of users. Grow or die. So, I picked up some old books and started transcribing them. You know, appeal to new niche demographics. I had the magic books. I had some polo books. Can you believe there isn't a bigger audience that's hungry for polo slang? It's tragic. But it didn't work. The app didn't grow. 18 months of my life wasted and now I have to start over. No, really. I'm not bitter."

"And when you were trying to blow life back into the frog?"

"Telemedicine!"

"You're going to put a video of reanimating the frog online?"

"No, no, no," The Founder was legitimately excited for a change. "Online healthcare is getting lots of investment money right now. If the chanting actually works, then I can digitize it. And patent it. And then sell it online. Do you know how valuable resurrections could be during an outbreak? No doctors, no hospitals, no overhead. Just a server and the patient's credit card."

"If you got the spell out of a book, isn't that what the lawyers call prior art? I don't think you can patent something that already exists."

"And that is why you raise enough investment money to hire good lawyers," The Founder was growing manic. "It's not something you have to worry about if you can outspend whoever's challenging your patent."

"Yeah, let's talk about that. Somebody's already challenging your patent."

"That's crazy," The Founder paused to step on another ant that had climbed out of the grass. "You can't challenge something before it's filed. Wait. Did somebody file a patent before I can figure out how this works?"

"No," Mister Lewis stared down at The Founder and frowned. "A successfully reanimated body trashed your old office. Twice."

The Founder was quiet for a change.

"The first time," Mister Lewis continued, "somebody spoke through the corpse and demanded that your successor 'cleanse the text.' Are you following me? You're not the only one with a spell book and that's a community that values secrecy. Do you think you might have attracted some attention you can't handle?"

"You're joking."

"I'm not."

"Then what did the corpse say the second time one trashed the office?"

"Nothing. I lit it on fire before it had a chance to talk."

The Founder stared at Mister Lewis for two long minutes, looking for a smile or another sign of a prank being played. There was no such sign, save for the slight raising of a mildly annoyed eyebrow.

"The first one spoke?" The Founder's voice had doubt for the first time.

"That's right. And you made whoever reanimated it, probably multiple people that reanimated it, angry. Is your clue light coming on yet? I need some answers about where you got those spellbooks."

"I thought I already killed those ants?"

The Founder was staring at the ground and two ants had crawled up out of the grass. The Founder raised a foot and stomped on them, grinding the heel to ensure the deed was done.

"It would be very hard for you to have killed them," came a small, deep voice from behind The Founder and Mister Lewis.

The pair whirled, but no one was there. And then they noticed movement on the ground. The dead frog was picking itself up from where The Founder threw it and rocking back into a sitting position.

"Take another look," instructed the frog. "The ants were already dead."

"Back up," ordered Mister Lewis as he retreated a step, but The Founder paid him no heed.

Upon closer examination, the ants looked desiccated. Not all of their legs worked, but the ants stumbled forward anyway. Dead ants were coming to the surface with increasing frequency.

"Time to leave," yelled Mister Lewis, but The Founder was frozen.

The ants sped up and climbed atop each other, forming a pulsating curtain between Mister Lewis and The Founder.

"I wouldn't touch the ants," said the frog. "Siafu ants are known for their bite and they haven't fed since... they were alive."

"The text is being cleansed," shouted Mister Lewis through the wall of ants. "They're deleting everything off the servers. You don't need to do this."

On the other side of the curtain of ants, the frog hopped onto The Founder's foot. The Founder stayed frozen.

"You understand our wisdom is not meant for the unwashed masses," the frog said to The Founder. It was not a question.

The Founder said nothing.

"You understand that accidents happen when novices play games with such knowledge," again the frog was not asking a question.

The Founder said nothing.

"You will tell us who you stole those tomes from," the frog grew irritated.

The Founder said nothing.

"You will tell us where you are keeping those tomes," the frog hopped backwards off The Founder's foot.

"Information wants to be free," muttered the petulant Founder. "You can't contain information that's been released into the wild."

"Information wants to be contained," said the frog. "Information belongs to those who can understand it.

You, especially, can be contained. And you will be contained before your reckless attempt to profit off the hidden knowledge causes a plague of the undead. You play with unleashing a zombie hoard to devour humanity with your ignorance, so shall you be devoured."

The curtain of ants fell on The Founder and what mandibles were left on those ants started chewing. It took about 5 minutes before The Founder stopped screaming. There was enough meat left on the bones for the body to be almost recognizable. The final blow was dealt by ants eating their way through the ear canal into the skull cavity.

"Was that absolutely necessary?" Mister Lewis asked the frog.

"You're no virgin," replied the frog. "You know that examples must be made when a protocol breach of this magnitude has occurred."

"So be it," sighed Mister Lewis. "I acknowledge the problem and was attempting to contain it. The kid wasn't my client, just someone with more ambition than experience. Do we have a beef?"

"You have understood the gravity of the situation," said the frog. "You have taken the initial steps to contain, even if you were slow to deal with the instigator."

"Never mind what I do or do not find an appropriate punishment, it was not my place to be an executioner today."

"True. The punishment is more official if it is we who make the example."

"Is there going to be a problem between you and my employer?" asked Mister Lewis.

"Will the text be cleansed?" asked the frog in return.

"The parts they control will be. You saw whose doing this was. Steps will be taken."

"And the parts they cannot control?" asked the frog.

"We may all have gotten lucky there," Mister Lewis attempted to sound reassuring. "The knowledge wasn't uploaded to a popular website. It was a crappy little app with a crappy little website. It's not immediately clear the website was popular enough to be backed up. Most people wouldn't know what they were looking at in the context of a slang app. There's every chance it wasn't even noticed in the first place."

"You will ensure they cleanse the text?" asked the frog.

"I am retained to resolve the situation," said Mister Lewis. "I don't want necromantic rituals floating around for the public to mangle any more than you do. What can be done will be done. My client wants no trouble and already severed ties with... the deceased."

"We will call it a truce for the time being," said the frog. "Go and see to the cleansing. We would dislike having to make a more public display, so all would be well were it handled quietly. If you locate the tomes, bring them to this spot. We will know that you left them. Otherwise, we shall start looking for them ourselves. This rabble really isn't worth the time and energy to reanimate for such simple questions."

A line of dead ants marched in the direction of The Founder's house to start that search, leaving a trail of blood behind them as though they were drawing a line from owner to property. Mister Lewis took care to keep his shoes clean as he left the backyard.

Transmigrate and Chill

1. The Threesome Wedding

"You may kiss the bride," said The Reverend.

And so, The Groom did. Then his eyes went wide with shock. His Bride's tongue surprised him. It wasn't so much that the tongue was doing the impossible, so much as it was doing something out of character and in a very specific, very personal way. His Bride's tongue was maneuvering exactly like the tongue of someone he had thought he'd escaped.

The Groom withdrew, confused and disturbed that such a memory would resurface immediately after saying "I do." The Bride glanced up and flashed a smile. The wrong smile. An all too familiar smile that belonged with that dancing tongue.

"No," whispered The Groom, hoping he was imagining things, but knowing deep down that he wasn't.

"I told you I'd marry you," The Bride managed to look sinister while beaming. "Love always finds a way."

"How?" began the groom, but his voice trailed off.

"I have no idea," replied The False Bride. "I woke up and suddenly I looked like this. It's our destiny. Our love willed it into being and the universe provided."

The Groom went pale. He opened his mouth to protest, but words failed him. So, he closed his mouth and ran for the exit.

"I'm not as pretty when I'm her," The False Bride glanced down at herself. "The sacrifices you make for love..."

2. Liability

"I'm sorry to drag you in again so soon," began The Investor. "We're looking at the most absurd class action lawsuit I've ever seen, and it falls into your area. I'm almost starting to think my apps are cursed."

"More reanimated bodies?" asked Mister Lewis, slightly alarmed. "Was someone killed? I thought you were able to remove those texts from the server before more damage was done. Was there an archive?"

"We did scrub the app and there don't appear to be any archives. OK, the Internet Archive had something up, but there was a helpful fellow there who scrubbed it in exchange for some rare comic books. I'm good at cutting deals. This is about a dating app I invested in. The bodies aren't dead, but there seem to be different people inhabiting them. Some kind of mind swap. It's got to be related."

"Are you talking transmigration?" asked Mister Lewis.

"I don't know what that means," replied The Investor. "This is what I know: some semi-slick personal injury lawyer has started a class action lawsuit. He's already got two incidents he's suing for and he's looking for more people to add. Both times, the weird magic-y thing happened after people were using a dating app in my investment portfolio. In the first incident, somebody got married and his ex-girlfriend was allegedly in the body of his bride. The ex-girlfriend isn't complaining, it sounds like she wanted to get married, but the original bride's now in the ex-girlfriend's body and she wants blood. Then we've got another case of a man and a woman switching bodies. The woman was fairly wealthy and the guy now inhabiting her body is spending all her money. The lawyer claims in each incident, the last thing the offended party remembered before waking up in a new body was using that dating app."

"Slow down. You said nobody died?"

"Not that anyone has reported. My understanding is all the parties are in good physical health."

"If nobody died, it's unlikely to be necromancy. There's a difference between reanimating a corpse and a soul switching bodies. Implanting a soul in a new body is called transmigration. Totally different field of practice. Those were necromancers that were upset about their arts getting floated on a website with amateurish edits."

"Does that exclude them from knowing other magic?" asked The Investor.

"Not in theory," replied Mister Lewis. "But that's not how it usually works. Especially since they were acting in a punitive fashion. Their interest was in punishing the person responsible for... we'll call it leaking classified information. I don't agree with their methods, but they weren't wrong about that being dangerous material to float around in public. If they were looking to punish you, it's unlikely they'd try something indirect and from a different school of sorcery. These are folks who want you to know why the two-ton weight is falling from the sky before it hits you."

"Did you ever figure out who they were?"

"More like a general idea of what they are, than who they are. If they don't want their identities known, it would be very expensive to find out. They wouldn't appreciate my looking and the odds are they'd find out about it. You're much better off saving your money and pretending it never happened."

"That could be difficult," sighed The Investor. "I've already got a lawsuit filed against me over that."

"From what angle?" asked Mister Lewis.

"A wrongful death suit filed by The Founder's Father. He's alleging I caused the death by creating an un-healthy work environment. Too many hours, too much stress. Thinks we cheated our way into diluting out The Founder's shares of the company. Which is crazy. Everything we did is standard practice in the startup world. And there's no way that body looks like a suicide."

"Posting those spells online was pretty close to sui-cide, but I don't think the kid knew any better. I suppose it's not my place to say what factors contributed to that decision."

"This is how it works," explained The Investor with a slight eye roll. "Everyone in the Venture Capital game likes to invest in startup founders who are a little crazy. And when I say a little crazy, I mean like obsessive-com-pulsive disorder crazy. If they're OCD, they stay at work and you get an extra ten or twenty hours of work out of them each week without paying extra for it. You know they'll leave no stone unturned because they won't want to admit they're wrong or that they failed. You don't want to invest in someone who's too crazy, because then things just turn toxic, and the other employees quit. But the ones who are just a little crazy, they're a value investment and half the time they're too eager for a deal and don't bother sending their paperwork to a lawyer. It's much easier to get rid of them if they screw up or if the startup gets too big for them to handle when they take the initial paperwork as-is and don't insist on building protections into the deal. The trouble is when they're really obsessed and full of irrational self-confidence, they sometimes come unraveled if things don't go their way. It's an occupational hazard. Investing goes on, startup founders sometimes don't."

"So, your lawyers are used to replacing the cogs in your startup machines... by force if necessary."

"We only need about one out of ten startups to hit big. If the other nine bust, we still make money. That said, it's better to sell off the other nine before they go bust. Sometimes you need to get rid of a founder to get the startup ready for sale. OK, you don't really sell the company, so much as you sell the remaining team. You sell it to a bigger company doing similar work and say, 'these guys have a track record in your business – buy them and make them build your next product.' I get my money back and sometimes a tiny profit. If the founders did the paperwork right, they might get a little cash from the sale. The employees get raises and velvet handcuffs."

"So, you're effectively selling indentured servitude?"

"Extremely well-paid indentured servitude. They can get double their normal salary. It's the only skin trade that's still legal because they can make so much money from the arrangement. Hardly anyone quits until they've had their fill lining up at the trough and it makes the economy go round. But when we have lawsuits, it hurts the ability to sell these companies or even have an IPO. That is, unless I can find a way to get a lot of free publicity off the lawsuits and jack up the user bases from the notoriety. Until I can find a way to turn this class action suit into a landslide of new customers, I need to figure out what's causing this mind swapping. It's more important to stop it than it is to know who's doing it, short term. If you can reverse it, or just stop it from happening again, my lawyers can handle the suit. The whole suit sounds ridiculous... the idea of having liability for marrying the wrong person in the right body... but if there are three more of those, it could cost a lot of money to settle."

"Do we at least know if the transmigrated people were in the same location when it happened?" asked Mister Lewis.

"They were not," replied The Investor.

"That's very, very hard to do at a distance."

"So, bigwigs like the necro-whatsits did this! See? I told you it was related."

"Look, I can examine the people and see if there's any lingering evidence of transmigration. There may or may not be detectable indications of what transpired, but I'll look. Either way, this doesn't feel like the same people are after you."

3. The Law for Fun and Profit

"This could cost you a lot of money," said The Lawyer.

"I think we first need to establish what transpired," replied Mister Lewis.

"I have a convenient list of what happened," said The Lawyer, picking up a legal pad covered in quasi-legible handwriting. "Aiding and abetting marriage under false pretenses. Identity theft. Aiding and abetting the misappropriation of funds through identity theft. Pain and suffering due to becoming a different person. Pain and suffering due to the misappropriation of money. Pain and suffering due to someone else spending your money. We're probably looking at mental anguish in perpetuity, fearing that it could all happen again. Your company has been very naughty and it's time to pay up."

"Are you talking about criminal charges or civil charges?" asked Mister Lewis. "I think you might be mixing your accusations a little too freely."

"My clients reserve the right to pursue criminal charges in the event that a settlement cannot be reached," huffed the lawyer. "Why, we might even take you to ecclesiastical court over this."

"I don't think an ecclesiastical court is going to have the authority to level the monetary damages you're concerned with, but it might be an appropriate venue to arbitrate whether the souls were married or just the bodies... assuming you can establish that there really were souls in the wrong bodies. But let's cut to the chase: how did you arrive at the conclusion that a dating app caused minds and bodies to swap? Don't you think that's a little farfetched?"

"Detective work," beamed The Lawyer. "First, a long-time client came in after his disastrous wedding."

"Yes," replied Mister Lewis. "I heard all about The Groom and his False Bride."

"Naturally, to determine if it was a prank, I contacted his ex-fiancée. And it turned out she was The Real Bride. And she was upset to be wearing someone else's body."

"This still sounds like an elaborate practical joke to me, but pray continue."

"And she told us that the last thing she remembered was being on her bachelorette party the night before. Her bridesmaids wanted her to revisit her options with the dating app she met The Groom on. She logged in and... next thing she knew, she wasn't herself and she was in someone else's home."

"The False Bride's home."

"That's correct. The home of the body she now inhabits. She's terribly upset about this. We could probably settle her portion of the suit right now for two million."

Mister Lewis frowned and paused before replying.

"And that's just assuming she stays in the alleged other body?"

"Heavens, no," the lawyer laughed. "That's the pain and suffering. It's really degrading. She doesn't think much of her rival's looks. There's an entirely different settlement on the table if her looks have been permanently downgraded."

"Right. So, let's get back to how you came to blame the app for this. Surely you've got more proof than one person's story?"

"Naturally. Not an hour later, I had another longtime client contact me. Only now she was a he. And I don't mean surgery was involved."

"So, your client was in another man's body?" asked Mister Lewis.

"She was. And this guy is a Big Spender. Come to find out, The Big Spender didn't have a problem wearing a new body. She, I mean he, likes having money. My client inherited a considerable sum and was always a Big Saver. The Big Spender's been on a shopping spree. Now, you realize that if we can't return the merchandise when this is over, your company will be liable for the funds that were illicitly spent."

"It's not my company," sighed Mister Lewis. "They're a client, just like you have clients. And I suppose your Big Saver can't remember anything after logging into the dating app?"

"Not a thing until she woke up as someone else. How did you guess?"

"And your clients... they're acquainted with each other?"

"What does that have to do with anything?" The Lawyer looked taken aback. "I have monthly parties for clients. It's a legitimate business write-off. They mingle. I can't say I recall if they've ever spoken."

"Right. And The Big Spender... 'he' remembers nothing after using the dating app?"

"I have no idea," the lawyer avoided eye contact. "We're still trying to get into the house. The police are not being very accommodating in this matter."

"Reporting someone for living in their own house usually doesn't draw the SWAT team. And this is the basis of your complaint? Two people claiming to be someone else. No forensics? That's it?"

"Naturally, when we discovered the pattern, we put out our feelers. Our paralegals are currently vetting numerous individuals who may have been afflicted by that dangerous app. You really should shut it down until we've reached a settlement."

"Tell you what, I'm going to vet your existing clients for you and maybe, just maybe, I'll discover what's really going on here."

"You're going to tell us how my clients switched bodies through the magic of technology?" asked The Lawyer.

"Technology? No. But if it was magic, I suspect I'll find out. Assuming your clients aren't merely well coached in each other's personal histories."

"My firm has never been successfully prosecuted for falsifying witness statements," screamed The Lawyer as Mister Lewis walked out the door.

4. The Metaphysics of Matrimony

"I don't think It is taking visitors today." While The Groom had somewhat recovered from the shock ending of his wedding, his mood was souring like a lemonade factory that ran out of sugar.

"That's alright," said Mister Lewis. "Being obnoxious is part of my job. I don't mind barging in on her. Before I do that, you're absolutely positive she's not your Bride anymore? That she couldn't be faking it, and this isn't just some sort of prank that's gotten way out of hand?"

"Nobody else is that good at pushing my buttons," replied The Groom. "It's no act. She was herself the night before the wedding when she left for the bachelorette party and the next time I saw her was at the ceremony and... she was... It. I'm supposed to have a restraining order and I can't get it enforced because now she looks like my Bride. The cops think I'm insane."

"Technically speaking," began Mister Lewis, "this would normally fall under fraud enforcement in secular policing..."

He was interrupted by a doorbell.

The Groom's eyes shot to the door, the way that only happens when nerves are frayed. He paused, shrugged his shoulders and walked over to peek through the peephole.

"So," The Groom said slowly, "if there's a False Bride in my Bride's body, is it likely that my Bride is in the False Bride's body?"

"It's theoretically possible," replied Mister Lewis. "Your lawyer claimed to have spoken with her and believes that to be the case."

"So, there's no chance that my Bride isn't just gone and I'm stuck with two of... her? Keeping me isolated and surrounded sounds just like why I left my ex."

"Anything is possible until we've established the facts. Perhaps you should let her in, and we can start establishing those facts?"

And so, The Groom opened the door and, in the doorway, stood the body of his former fiancée, perhaps now occupied by his intended bride, her arms outstretched in search of a hug. She didn't get that hug as the groom recoiled and retreated.

"Don't be that way," she said. "It's not my fault she did this to me. I'm starting to think you weren't exaggerating about her."

The Groom took another step back.

"Perhaps you can tell him something his ex- wouldn't know?" sighed Mister Lewis.

"He likes bananas in his cornflakes," she offered.

"I've liked bananas in my cornflakes since I was 6 years old," stammered The Groom. "All kinds of people know that."

"Perhaps something from the last week," said Mister Lewis. "Before the wedding. Any private plans you hadn't shared?"

"The mangos?" her voice was tentative.

"Oh," The Groom blushed.

"I'll take it that works for you," said Mister Lewis.

"Um, yes," stammered The Groom. "Look, your matron of honor told me you were fooling around with that dating app and you weren't the same afterwards."

"First off," began the True Bride, "That app was her idea, not mine. But yes, she insisted I see who else I matched with. It was that or a "suck for a buck" necklace and... ugh... you know what the girls are like on bachelorette parties. I remember logging in and then next thing I knew, I looked like this."

"I don't think I like that app," muttered The Groom.

"But baby, that app is how I found you."

The Groom's blush deepened and the two embraced.

"Some things never change," came a voice from the back of the room. The False Bride had deigned to make an appearance. "You still look good in my arms. I apologize for looking like her. It really is a step down but being together is the most important thing."

And thus, the hug was broken up.

"I guess we have something in common, after all," she directed the comment at her former body. "That app is how I found my love, too. Perhaps it should have stopped after perfection, though."

"So, you two agree about using the app," interjected Mister Lewis.

"Who exactly is he?" The False Bride pointed an accusatory finger.

"He's from the dating app," blurted The Groom. "He's here to fix everything that's happened."

"Let's not get ahead of ourselves," said Mister Lewis. "First, I need to determine that something happened in the first place. Pardon my suspicious nature."

"Our fate happened," The False Bride raised her chin and stuck a pose of superiority. "All you have to do is believe."

"Are you referring to Kraft and Macht?" Mister Lewis produced a monocle from his pocket and started slowly looking The False Bride's Body over from head to toe while peering through its lens.

"Kraft," stammered The False Bride. "It was my will that brought us back together, not macaroni and cheese. My will and the universe providing for us."

"Kraft and Macht," began Mister Lewis as he stood up and lowered the monocle, "translates roughly to force and might. Their relationship establishes Nietzsche's concept of will to power. I really wish these modern self-help books would acknowledge where they get their ideas from."

Mister Lewis raised the monocle again and started examining The True Bride's Body.

"Are you denying the universe works magic?" The False Bride demanded with all due volume.

"I would never deny that," Mister Lewis straightened up and returned the monocle to his pocket. "I'm just not seeing any magic at work here. I'm afraid there's nothing I can do about this... situation."

The Groom was silent as Mister Lewis left. His once and future brides, less so.

5. Other People's Money

The gate was open at the mansion as Mister Lewis approached. At first glance, it looked to be the sort of gate that was opened and closed electronically. It was the sort of gate that was intended to remain shut when not admitting a very specific visitor. After all, a gate left open could let in the riffraff.

Nothing stirred on the estate as he walked up the empty driveway. Reaching the front door... or at least he thought it was the front door and not the servant's entrance... he rang the bell. He didn't wait long before a rail thin middle-aged woman opened the door.

"Where's the pizza?" the woman rasped. She glanced about furtively, as though something was out of place. "I left the gate open. You didn't need to park on the street."

"I don't think that's the type of gate that gets left open," Mister Lewis suppressed an eye roll.

"That gate really sticks when you pull on it. But where's the pizza?"

"I think you might have me confused for someone else," Mister Lewis noticed the woman's sweatsuit was mismatched. The hoodie and pants were both clearly expensive, but each was a different color and from a different designer. "I'm with the dating app. There were some complaints I'm here to look into."

The woman tried to slam the door, but Mister Lewis had his foot in the way.

"That's not very friendly," continued Mister Lewis. "But this doesn't have to take long. I understand you were using our dating app a couple days ago and then experienced some changes? Is that the story?"

"I don't know what you're talking about. I'm experiencing true happiness on my own. If you don't have my pizza, go away!"

Breaks squealed as a car with a delivery sign on the roof careened into the driveway behind Mister Lewis, the driver's eyes darting around the way eyes sometimes do when trying to make a promised delivery time while avoiding a fifth moving violation.

"If you want your pizza, you're going to have to come out and play," Mister Lewis smiled as he blocked the door.

The woman glared as her eyes tracked the teenager in the pizza delivery t-shirt exiting the car, holding a pizza box.

"Have it your way," she sighed.

The woman opened the door. Mister Lewis backed up and swept his arm in a gesture of safe passage. She stepped forward past Mister Lewis and snatched the pizza box out of the teenager's hands. When she turned back, she found her path to the doorway blocked.

"Aren't you forgetting something?" croaked the teenager.

The woman turned and glared in reply, prompting the teenager to sulk back into the car and drive off. As the car cleared the gate, the woman turned back to the mansion and glared at the obstacle between her and the front door.

"Were you planning on closing the gate?" asked Mister Lewis. "Probably shouldn't leave it open like that. You could shut it the same way you opened it... or perhaps you'll remember where the remote control is?"

The woman's glare intensified.

"Either way, we need to talk about this complaint the app got about you not being you. It's OK. I don't mind if you eat while we talk."

The woman opened the pizza box, pulled out a slice and started chewing. She didn't speak.

"What do you think you're putting into my mouth?" came a gravelly voice from down the driveway. A disheveled man in worn sweatpants was crossing through the gate. The man would have been round, were it not for the way every part of his body sagged.

The pizza went down the wrong pipe and the woman started coughing. Mister Lewis couldn't be sure if her eyes were bugging out and watering because of the effort to dislodge the food from her windpipe or it was shock, but there definitely had been a reaction to the new visitor.

"It's not bad enough you're trying to remake my figure into your image," wheezed the man, slightly winded by the walk up the driveway. "Now you're trying to choke me to death? Please. If you want to kill yourself, do it in your own body. God knows you've been laying the groundwork for an early grave."

Still coughing, the woman squared to face the man and started backing towards the door.

"What are you wearing?" continued the man. "I don't own track clothes, and if I did, I'm more than capable of matching tops and pants. How much more of my money have you been wasting lowering my wardrobe to your slovenly standards?"

The man gestured towards his decidedly lower market sweats and winced before turning to Mister Lewis.

"And who are you supposed to be?" the man continued. "Don't tell me you're the new butler."

"I believe your lawyer told you I'd be here," replied Mister Lewis.

"You're from the app?"

"I am. Would you mind telling me exactly what happened?"

"I'll tell you what I remember," the man scratched his head. "Then maybe you can tell me what happened. It doesn't make a lot of sense. I'd opened the app and updated my photos. That was all normal. Then I decided to finally do the full personality scan. One minute I was staring into my phone and I was me. The next, I was staring into someone else's phone in this body."

"I thought I was the only one," murmured the woman.

"Now we're getting somewhere," Mister Lewis turned, a smile on his face that was not altogether kind. "So, you do have something to share?"

The woman reverted to glaring and said nothing.

"He's wearing my body and spending my money," screamed the man. "I know my bank login. I can see exactly how much he's spending and where. If you don't get me out of this body and back into my own soon, he'll have me looking like him. I know where he's been ordering takeout from. I see all the bank transactions. It's disgusting. He doesn't tip, either."

"If things are as you describe," began Mister Lewis, "we still don't have a confirmation as to who's inhabiting your original body. You're making an assumption of a one-to-one personality swap. That's not always the case with transmigration. There's also the small matter of verifying that such a thing has occurred."

They both turned to stare at the woman, who started inching backwards toward the door.

"Fine," sighed Mister Lewis. "Let's get a look at you."

Mister Lewis produced the monocle from his pocket and peered through it at the woman's head. Then her back. The woman didn't stop backing up as he did this. He stepped aside as she backed through the door and was gazing at her front torso as the door slammed in his face.

"What are you doing?" asked the man.

"This is a gadget that helps detect... emissions," Mister Lewis turned and began to repeat the process on the man. "I'm looking for evidence that your body has had outside forces acting on it, evidence of changes, that sort of thing."

"What branch of science does this fall under?"

"Easiest to just call it physics," Mister Lewis frowned. "That said, I'm not seeing any... unusual readings off either of you."

"You can't possibly be trying to tell me nothing is wrong here," the man struck an indignant pose.

"No, something certainly seems off. I won't deny that. But whatever it is may not be what was described to me when I was sent here. I'll continue to make inquiries."

6. Better Dating Through Science

The Chief Dating Officer was about what you'd expect for someone with that title: young, irrationally confident and inexperienced in dating.

"I've heard of you," The CDO was almost hyperventilating. "You were fighting zombies in our sister-app's office last week."

"Your Investor has me looking into some irregularities with your app users," replied Mister Lewis.

"Are zombies starting to use our apps?" The CDO's enthusiasm knew no boundaries. "We can optimize an experience for them. Do zombies have different relationship interests than the living?"

"Zombies really only have the interests their masters give them," Mister Lewis shrugged and whispered. "I'm here about the possible transmigration incidents."

The CDO stared blankly in reply.

"The mind swapping."

"Oh," some recognition glinted in The CDO's eyes. "You mean that's not a scam?"

"I'm not sure yet," said Mister Lewis. "There are some awfully good, well-coordinated actors involved if it's a scam. That said, I'm not seeing what I'd expect to be seeing if there were transmigrations."

"What would you expect to see?"

"Evidence of magic in play."

"How do you find magic?" The CDO was getting excited again. "Hey, I bet we could make a great app for that. People would pay for a magic detector."

"You let me worry about the magic," Mister Lewis winced as he spoke. "Just because I wasn't seeing it, doesn't mean it wasn't manifesting in an unusual way. I need you to explain to me exactly how your app works. I'm looking for potential triggers, so a detailed explanation is preferable."

"We mostly use the standard algorithms," began The CDO. "Collaborative filtering. The user makes selections, and we narrow their choices based on who they click. And then we find other users who click on some of the same people and put some of those choices in the viewing queue."

"You're not doing personality questions?" asked Mister Lewis. "Compatibility ratings? That sort of thing?"

"Sure," shrugged The CDO. "It's all fairly standard psychology surveys. I mean, we rewrite them and make them a little less stiff. It gives the users a compatibility score and thins out matches for deal breakers, but... it's a dating app. Dating apps are about the pictures. Our data suggests the users don't really pay attention to the compatibility score. It's not necessarily predictive of a relationship. Unless you're talking about the special project. We have high hopes for that, but it's new and we don't have enough data in to know if it actually works."

"If these people aren't scammers, then something special is going on, all right. Keep talking."

"It's a personality scan," said The CDO.

Now it was time for Mister Lewis to give a blank stare.

"We're partnered with another startup for it," continued the Chief Dating Officer. "I can't really explain the mechanics of it, but the user stares into the camera and the flash goes off in precise, coded bursts and the app scans their brain and pulls out the answers for the compatibility test. Something to do with pupil response. I'm really more on the marketing side of the business. Anyway, it theoretically gives us more accurate answers than just having the user fill out the form. Unless, you know, the user is lying to themself."

"That's definitely different," Mister Lewis paused. "And this was all arrived at with science? No strange ancient books?"

"I guess some of the psychology books are old," offered The CDO. "But everything on our side of it's pretty standard. Dating apps are mostly all the same under the hood. Everyone differentiates with their branding and their user interface. And I don't think our partner's using anything except code."

"Can you pull up your records on the alleged victims?" asked Mister Lewis.

"Easy."

"These three were the first group," Mister Lewis handed The CDO a slip of paper. "The two women both claimed to have matched with that man. The first one was supposed to marry him. The second one is the ex-girlfriend who allegedly swapped bodies with the finance."

"Say, that's really rare," The CDO looked up from a smartphone. "Both of those ladies are a 100% match with that guy using the personality scan method."

"The one claiming to be his ex- did say they were a perfect match," snorted Mister Lewis.

"They should be," The CDO nodded. "At least that's how the model works, and we have every reason to believe it's accurate. Still, you know how it is in real life? Sometimes if people are too much alike... we haven't determined if we need to cap compatibility at 98% or not."

"Let's see if that's a coincidence," Mister Lewis hand-ed The CDO another slip. "These two claim to have swapped bodies... or at least one of them does. The one who's currently a woman let slip he used the app, but clammed up pretty tight about everything else. If there's a love triangle, nobody's realized it yet."

The CDO stroked the smartphone and furrowed a brow.

"It's the same thing," The CDO sat on the edge be-tween confused and astonished. "Both people 100% matched on the same woman... but... it doesn't look like there was ever a date. She never responded to either of them. We should probably try to prompt a date. Having 100% matches meet in person is vital to validating our data model."

"I take it, it's unusual for me to randomly encounter two pairs of matches like this?"

"Obviously not statistically impossible if it happened, but close to it. I should probably start flagging these in the system."

"Worry about that a little later," Mister Lewis nar-rowed his eyes. "Is your system set up where you could manually set a match to 100% so we can test this?"

"You mean like a control group?"

"Exactly like a control group."

"Do you want me to put you in the system?"

"No," said Mister Lewis. "If a transmigration happens, I need to be monitoring the event to see how it's happening and figure out if there's a way to counteract it. If my soul goes travelling, I might not be aware what's happening until it's over."

"Um, OK," The CDO was getting hesitant. "If you give me a minute, I can set it up so our Cash Extraction Officer and I are 100% matched on the same person."

"You've both used the app?"

"Of course."

"And you've both done the personality scan before?"

"Sure. You ready for me to save the new settings?"

Mister Lewis pulled the monocle from his pocket and raised it.

"Go for it."

The CDO tapped the smartphone. Neither person moved for a moment.

"I think I'm still me," said The CDO. "What's with the monocle?"

"Think of it as a type of smart glasses," said Mister Lewis. "Are you logged into your personal account in the app or administrator?"

"Good point," The CDO fumbled with the smart phone. "Aaaaaaaand... I'm still me."

"And your boss?"

The CDO pulled up the smartphone's contact list, dialed and put it on speaker.

"Hello," said the speaker.

"Where are you at?" asked The CDO.

"I'm in the server room," said The Cash Extraction Officer. "Why?"

"The app might have a bug with the personality scan," replied The CDO. "Could you log in to your account?"

"Fine," and The CEO hung up.

The CDO fiddled with the smartphone again.

"Records have updated with a log in and rescan of the personality," said The CDO.

Mister Lewis opened his mouth to ask a question but was interrupted as the door burst open and The CEO came crashing into the room.

"How did I get in the server," began The CEO before freezing midsentence and staring slack jawed at The CDO. "Why are there two of me?"

Mister Lewis and The CDO exchanged a glance.

"And who are you supposed to be?" Mister Lewis asked The CEO.

"I'm the Chief Dating Officer," replied The CEO's now occupied body. "Who are you and who's my clone?"

"How long since you did a personality scan?" Mister Lewis asked The CDO.

"Maybe a couple weeks?"

"If this works the way I think it does, that means your boss is now you... but you from two weeks ago," Mister Lewis turned and approached The CEO, monocle up. "Your Investor sent me over to check out a bug in your app. That's why you're feeling disoriented."

"Did I match with myself?" asked The CEO's body.

"I always did find myself attractive," said The CDO. "Does this mean it's not really a body swap?"

"No," answered Mister Lewis. "Your soul didn't go anywhere. I have no idea what this is. You said you partnered with another company for this personality scan?"

"Yes," said both CDOs in unison.

"It's another startup in our Investor's portfolio," continued the original CDO.

"We're encouraged to share resources," interjected The CEO's body.

"Their office is in the basement," the two CDOs blurted out in tandem.

7. Sufficiently Advanced Technology

As advertised, the office was underground. It was a modest office. A few scattered desks in the "open office style" that offered investors savings on furniture and casual surveillance while rewarding employees with added noises and distractions. This open office was quiet. Only one employee was present.

"Can I help you?" asked The Data Guru.

"I sure hope so," Mister Lewis gestured to The CEO and CDO. "Would you be able to explain why there are two of them?"

"I beg your pardon?" asked The Data Guru.

"You're partnered with their dating app?"

"I am."

"There have been some complaints about the app. People claiming their mind has switched bodies after using the app. The CDO here – the one on the right – determined the people claiming to have swapped bodies all had a 100% match in common. So, we reset the database so The CDO and CEO would be a 100% match on the same person. After The CEO logged into the app and did one of your "personality scans," the CEO's personality seems to have been replaced with that of the

CDO. How can one person's mind be in two bodies? Can you explain that, please?"

"That's great," erupted The Data Guru. "It works! It actually works!"

"That's not really what I'd call an explanation," Mister Lewis loomed menacingly over The Data Guru. "I've got a body with the wrong consciousness in it. No souls moved. There was no transmigration of souls. How has the consciousness shifted? Elucidate. I'm not going to ask twice."

"Transmigration," The Data Guru seemed puzzled. "You mean like horror movie stuff?"

"Answer the question," growled Mister Lewis.

"Nothing's shifted... exactly," although The Data Guru was shifting from right foot to left and back. "It's hypnosis. When the user engages with the personality scan, a series of high-speed light impulses from the flash takes them under and..."

"Are you telling me you've been rewriting people's brains," interrupted Mister Lewis.

"Not so much rewriting as convincing them they're someone else."

"Are you saying this is reversible?"

"Absolutely. All you need to do is go back into the database and reset the 100% compatibility variable from 'transfer' to 'revert' and the next time they scan, they'll be back to normal."

"There's no variable like that," began The CDO.

"Wait a minute," interjected The CEO's body, "did you hack my app?"

"Why do you think I was paying you for the data?" sighed The Data Guru. "Did you not read the contract? Look, I can swap it from here."

The Data Guru sat down at a desk and pecked away at the keyboard. After a minute of typing, The Data Guru stood up and snatched The CEO's phone.

"This should fix you?" said The Data Guru, holding the phone to The CEO's face and tapping the screen.

The phone's camera flash broke into a rapid strobe pattern as The CEO stared, transfixed.

"Why am I in the basement?" asked The CEO after the light storm had passed.

"How did you do that?" asked The CDO.

"It's all about reapplication of the data," answered The Data Guru. "Adding my proprietary technology to your app, allows for a synergistic collection of..."

"The how is not the immediate concern," Mister Lewis interrupted. "Next question: how do we revert everyone else your 'experiment' has... displaced?"

"Yeah," agreed The CDO. "We should probably be doing that sooner than later."

"The variable's reset," said The Data Guru. "You just need to have them log into the app and scan themselves. You did keep a list of the 100% matches, didn't you?"

The CDO said nothing and fidgeted while avoiding eye contact.

"There's a better way," said Mister Lewis. "Broadcast an alert to every user that they have a new match. Require a scan to access it. Call it an update. That would cover you in case these hypnosis incidents have a wider scope, right?"

"I don't like your impugning the precision of my code," growled The Data Guru, "but that's fine."

"It leaves fewer fingerprints if it looks like a routine profile update," said Mister Lewis. "Your investor is going to want some plausible deniability on this. Send the alert and then double check to make sure any affected parties have scanned themselves and reverted to normal."

"I think I like that," said The CEO. "Is this part of your service?"

"My business card does have 'consultant' on it," replied Mister Lewis.

"Could you explain to me what we're establishing plausible deniability about?" asked The CEO.

"Tell you what," replied Mister Lewis. "We'll let your CDO set up that system alert and then you, me and The Investor are going to have a little chat about privacy agreements and liability."

Food Delivered

1. Dinner is Served

The doorbell rang.

The Financier opened the door and found what appeared to be a delivery driver waiting outside. The delivery driver said nothing but held up a smartphone with the Food Fling app displayed on the screen.

"You've got my moo shu pork?" asked The Financier.

The delivery driver remained silent.

"Do you have my dinner?" asked The Financier.

The delivery driver's face drew into a broad smile. As the smile widened, fangs slipped into view from beneath the parting lips.

"No," said the delivery driver. "I think you'll be the dinner, tonight."

The Financier stumbled backwards, eyes wide in confusion and apprehension.

The delivery driver stepped forward, paused at the doorway, chuckled and then stepped through.

The Financier kept backpedaling and stepped behind a large leather sofa, which the delivery person shoved across the room and out of the way with a flick of the wrist.

"You know I'm a big tipper, right?" The Financier gulped and produced a wad of bills from a pocket.

The delivery driver froze in place, the wide grin disappearing.

"Here. Just take my money."

The Financier tossed the wad of money in the direction of the delivery driver, the bills separating from the wad and scattering like a small green blizzard.

The delivery driver turned and ran.

Puzzled, The Financier slowly approached the door. Peering out, there was no trace of anyone in sight.

"What kind of freak runs away from money?" muttered the Financier while closing the door.

2. Steady Work

"I don't understand where all this is coming from," said The Investor, "but I might need to put you on staff full-time."

"Thank you, but no," replied Mister Lewis. "I'm much more comfortable as an independent consultant. Is there a new problem with The Founder's Father's lawsuit?"

"That was dismissed," The Investor smiled. "There is nothing that could be proved in court. Like I keep telling you, founders get removed from their company all the time. I can hardly be blamed for... how did he die again? It doesn't really matter. Our courts don't really have a precedent for people getting eaten by zombie ants."

"Those ants were a sort of court sentence," murmured Mister Lewis. "And that's a court you want to stay far clear of. But if we're not dealing with that, what's cropped up?"

"Anyway," The Founder resumed. "There's been a series of murders and the police think one of the companies I funded might be involved. 'Food Fling.' It's a food delivery app. Users of the app have been found dead with slit throats. Blood all over the place. The police think maybe somebody who works for the app is involved, since all the victims are customers. It's been a mystery, but after last night it's starting to sound like your kind of mystery. Somebody survived the last attack. Claims the delivery driver had fangs and chased the survivor back into the house before fleeing."

"Could be another fake," Mister Lewis paused. "Vampires don't enter homes uninvited."

"This is why you should work here full-time," reiterated The Investor. "You have a natural talent for disrupting lawsuits... in addition to handling the weird stuff."

"I work better when keeping my own counsel," offered Mister Lewis. "Fewer ethical entanglements, more business deductions. You're right to be concerned, though. It's highly improbable for three of your holdings to be involved in incidents with the appearance of unnatural influence in so short a time period. It seems suspicious."

"Vampires are undead, right?" asked The Investor. "Could this be those necrowhatsits coming back for seconds?"

"Necromancers," corrected Mister Lewis. "Technically, it's possible... but it doesn't usually work that way. Necromancers don't typically value free thought when they reanimate the dead and vampires tend to be independent thinkers that follow their own agendas. The two groups really don't get along very well. It would also be a lot more of an indirect approach than what we've already seen."

"But you're going to check and make sure whether this is a fake or the real thing?" asked The Investor. "Right now, this is just more bad publicity and I'm not seeing a good way to spin it. You ever hear about the Brown's

Chicken massacre? Murders are bad for the food business."

"My usual fee?" asked Mister Lewis.

"Of course," The Investor smiled wider. "Here's the address. Let me know what you find."

3. Delivery Refused

"**W**as this the first time you used the Food Fling app?" Mr. Lewis found himself at a large house on an upscale street. Not the sort of place one expects to find a slasher operating.

"No," answered The Financier. "But it was the first time I ever saw that delivery driver."

"At what point did you ask the driver inside?" asked Mr. Lewis.

"I didn't," replied The Financier. "I backed up through the front door and the driver just followed me in."

"Could you have motioned for the driver to enter?" asked Mr. Lewis.

"No," replied The Financier. "Absolutely not. Those teeth were creeping me out."

"And the attacker didn't say anything?" asked Mr. Lewis.

"Just that I was dinner," replied The Financier.

"How exactly did you get rid of the driver?" asked Mr. Lewis.

"I offered a bigger tip," replied The Financier.

"How did that work?" asked Mr. Lewis.

"Well, I reached into my pocket, grabbed my cash on hand and tossed it at the driver."

"That worked?"

"The driver left," The Financier's shoulders shrugged. "It was the damnedest thing though. The driver didn't take the money. Just ran away."

"You do that a lot? Throw money at things?"

"Well, not literally. That said, in my line of work, I'm a big believer in throwing money at problems."

"Thank you," said Mr. Lewis. "That might clear one or two things up. As you say, it's the damnedest thing."

4. Suspicious Minds

"The evidence is inconclusive," Mister Lewis had returned to The Investor's office. "But it's still possible that you have a vampire problem. While it makes no sense how a vampire could cross the threshold of a home uninvited, the reaction to money was consistent with a vampire encountering an object of belief. And the fangs, of course. Assuming they were real."

"Once more in English," said The Investor.

"Vampires have a problem with belief," explained Mister Lewis. "If a person believes in something strongly enough, it can cause the vampire physical harm. A small amount of belief can cause them pain or discomfort. Effectively, it keeps them off you. A large amount of belief can be like hitting them with a blowtorch. It can burn right through them if a person's belief is strong enough. Usually, belief has to be focused on an object to become weaponized. In traditional vampire lore, the crucifix is an object of belief. A person's belief does not grievously harm the vampire unless it's focused on the crucifix and the crucifix physically touches the vampire. A believer wearing a crucifix as a sign of faith, that's passive belief. It's not going to burn a vampire, but it will most likely keep the vampire off you. Grasp that same crucifix and focus your faith on it and touch the vampire with it, that's when the object of belief can do some damage. Might burn the vampire, might do worse. It really depends on how strongly the wielder believes. If that Financier believes in money enough and then produces a wad of bills, it could conceivably be just like a Christian holding a crucifix and that's why a vampire might have fled from the sight of money."

"That actually works?" asked The Investor.

"All manner of strange things work in the right context," replied Mister Lewis. "There are rules. It's just a matter of properly manipulating them."

"So, if I really like my cigar?" asked The Investor.

"There's a difference between liking and believing," explained Mister Lewis. "Sure, you might like a cigar, but do you believe in it? Does it define what you have faith in or how you live your life? There may be people where a cigar would be an object of faith, but you're not one of them. The Financier seems to have a life that revolves around money. He says he believes in throwing money at problems. That could be a glib saying or it could be central to his core being. Money could be what he believes in and a dollar bill could be symbolic of his faith. Informal monetary faiths and beliefs aren't unheard of in the greater scheme of things, but what the actual object of faith is can vary quite a bit from person to person. For example, someone who worships gold wouldn't be able to focus that kind of faith on a dollar bill. Perhaps a long time ago, but the dollar's no longer on the gold standard."

"Are you telling me the attempts to get the dollar back on the gold standard are because those people worship gold?" asked The Investor.

"Many things are possible," Mister Lewis smiled as he spoke. "Although if that's the case, the people pushing for it might not realize they're pushing for an article of faith. Almost everyone believes in something, but they don't always realize what it is. Self-awareness is optional with faith. So no, your cigar isn't going to ward off a nosferatu. On the other hand, having consulted for you, if you are confronted by a vampire, that money trick might work for you. It's worth trying in a pinch. But that's not the issue at hand. Right now, we need to test the hypothesis that your delivery drivers are involved in this. Have the police determined if there's a pattern to which drivers were scheduled opposite a murder?"

"It was always a new driver," said The Investor.

"Then I think we should go to your house and start placing some food orders," said Mister Lewis.

"My house?" asked The Investor.

"We need to get to the bottom of this business of whether you've got vampires crossing the threshold of a door and entering a home uninvited," explained Mister Lewis. "Vampires should not be able to cross a threshold, so either there's an imposter causing trouble or something very bad is happening with vampires. That would be bigger than your app being implicated and the members of my... community... would need to be informed. Vampires are invasive predators, and you can't have them out running around and feeding at will. It's a problem that can quickly get out of hand. A matter of public health, in a sense. We can't summon your delivery drivers here because an office isn't a home and effectively has no threshold. I also don't think it's a good idea to involve any of your Food Fling employees until we have a better idea what's going on and who might be involved. Besides, I don't live in your delivery area, so my place is out."

5. The Delivery Driver Never Rings Twice

Orders were placed and the food started to arrive. There hadn't been a pattern to the type of food involved with the murders, so Mister Lewis cast a wide net with both style and restaurant locations. The Investor begrudgingly conceded it was a sunk cost but found solace that both lunch and dinner for the next week could now be a tax-deductible business expense as the food was quickly shuttled to the refrigerator.

The first five deliveries were fairly normal. The sixth delivery was a little more... aggressive.

When the doorbell rang for the sixth delivery, Mister Lewis opened the door to find the delivery driver already crowding the door frame. Almost before the door was finished opening, a smile broke out on the delivery driver's face with a fang protruding from beneath the upper lip. A pigeon had come home to roost. An invasive pigeon with a taste for hemoglobin, but the desired pigeon, nonetheless.

Mister Lewis said nothing at the sight of the fang and merely took a step backwards to see what the delivery driver would do. Sure enough, the delivery driver stepped forward through the door and crossed the threshold as if there were nothing there.

"When exactly did I invite you in?" said Mister Lewis, a slight frown showing.

"It doesn't matter when, just that you did," the delivery driver hissed a bit too theatrically. "You were expecting me, weren't you?"

"How could I not be after yesterday?" Mister Lewis took another step backwards.

The delivery driver appeared puzzled and stopped advancing.

"I think we can both agree that was pretty sloppy," continued Mister Lewis. "Fleeing the scene of yesterday's delivery. Leaving a witness who saw your teeth. Raises all kinds of questions about what's been happening around here. Jeopardizes that carefully constructed slasher cover you had working for you. Inexcusably sloppy."

"You seem to have me mistaken for someone else," the delivery driver regained composure and returned the frown. "Rest assured, I'll ask around and find out who did that. That does sound sloppy... but I'll have dinner first."

The delivery driver stepped forward. Mister Lewis responded by slipping a thin silver chain out from inside his sleeve.

The delivery driver shot a claw of a hand towards Mister Lewis, diving for his throat. Taking an end of the chain in each hand, Mister Lewis stepped sideways and snared the delivery driver's wrist with the chain. The delivery driver made a choking noise and the exposed skin around the chain began to smoke. The delivery driver started to swing the opposite arm, but moved slowly, almost as though throwing a punch while underwater.

"Silver allergy acting up?" Mister Lewis asked in a tone not unlike a judge inquiring where a drunk and disorderly defendant's pants had gone to. "It's only going to get worse."

Mister Lewis stepped behind the delivery driver, pulling the wrist above the driver's shoulder before releasing one end of the chain and quickly whipping it around the driver's neck.

"Now let's go back to that thought you were so kind to share a moment ago," Mister Lewis grabbed the other end of the chain and started gently pulling back in a garroting motion. Once more, the delivery driver's skin started smoking where it touched the chain. "You said you were going to ask around about who'd been making deliveries last night and let their fangs get seen. How many friends of yours have been making food deliveries? Are you on a roster with a regular rotation?"

"I've got a better question," The Investor walked into the room. "Am I being targeted?"

The delivery driver's head slowly turned towards The Investor and then spat.

"Naughty," Mister Lewis pulled a bit tighter on the chain and more smoke spewed forth from where it dug into the delivery driver's neck. "Why don't you try answering in complete sentences?"

The delivery driver responded with another pained grunt.

"As long as you have it under control," began The Investor, "maybe we should find out about my belief in money? If that trick works, the driver will be uncomfortable enough to talk, right?"

"Might as well," agreed Mister Lewis. "If there are more of them, you might need something to protect yourself. Money's probably the most convenient thing for you if it works."

"Good," said The Investor, pulling out a stack of bills bound with a green strap. "I came prepared. You like two-dollar bills?"

The Investor waved the bills six inches from the driver's face. The driver winced in pain.

"What are you?" groaned the delivery driver. "Some kind of gospel of prosperity zealot?"

"Prosperity," growled The Investor. "Why don't you take a close look at my prosperity?"

The Investor tossed the stack of bills at the delivery driver, but instead of bouncing off the driver's chest, the bills melted right through leaving a hole. The bills bounced off Mister Lewis on the other side and left a smear of sludge that used to be part of the driver on his jacket before falling to the ground.

"Is it supposed to work like that?" asked The Investor.

Mister Lewis released the chain from around the delivery driver's neck and the body fell to the floor.

"It would seem you're a man of great convictions," Mister Lewis raised an eyebrow as he gazed down at the hole in the driver's chest.

"Will this work if the necromancers come for me?"

"On necromancers?" Mister Lewis looked up. "No. They're alive. That only really works on the undead. Certain types of them, at least. Mostly the sentient ones. Zombies are reanimated, but it won't have any effect on them. You also want to avoid eye contact with vampires. An object of belief will keep them off you, but it can't ward off mesmerism if you make the mistake of meeting one's gaze."

"So that delivery driver was a vampire?"

"Yes. And apparently there's a nest of them using the app."

"And it's dead now?"

"All vampires are dead, but that one is neutralized for the moment. I should probably remove the head for now. We can expose it to sunlight in the morning and scatter the ashes to make sure. Vampires have a nasty habit of reanimating if they aren't disposed of properly. You do know what this means, right?"

The Investor nodded no.

"We're going to need another vampire to interrogate."

6. Asking for Seconds

And so, the cycle of ordering food began again, although this time The Investor was a little less grumpy about spending the money on takeout while they sought another vampire infiltrating the service. Catching the first one was the proof of concept. Now they were entering a phase of continual improvement where they could apply the shared principles of Six Sigma and Lean management. Each time they uncovered another vampire posing as a delivery driver, they were entering a new iteration of an interrogation. They would apply insights gleaned from the previous interrogation and refine their technique until they had the perfect interrogation. At least that's how The Investor had been encouraged to approach it.

Mister Lewis was not viewing the evening's activities through quite the same lens. Oh, he was looking for insights, but the insights started with how to keep his client from accidentally destroying the next vampire before it could answer a few questions. All other insights would flow from there. Calling that an incremental improvement in the language of codified project management struck him as more pretentious than practical. Still, he was a consultant with a client and sometimes everything flowed smoother when the situation was translated into the client's language. Thus, they were taking a Lean and Agile approach to eliminating the vampire problem, just like any forward-thinking startup would tackle it. And that's how the billable hours would be written up on the invoice.

The first three deliveries were routine and produced a quantity of above average barbeque. It was the fourth delivery that allowed for the desired "continual improvement."

This time when Mister Lewis opened the door, the delivery driver was standing six inches outside and staring him in the face. Once again, instead of speaking, the driver simply stepped forward, pushing Mister Lewis back.

"You could introduce yourself," Mister Lewis said, stepping backwards to steer the brewing altercation.

The delivery driver kept pressing forward, chest to chest, until Mister Lewis was backed into a wall.

"You're a confident one, aren't you?" Mister Lewis gave a half nod to The Investor, who emerged from around a corner and quietly started dropping banded stacks of dollar bills in a semi-circle behind the delivery driver.

The delivery driver said nothing, preferring to pantomime a lazy yawn to better show the fangs. When Mister Lewis had no discernable reaction to the fangs, the puzzled driver paused.

"There's something wrong with you," said the delivery driver, eyes narrowing in concentration trying to discern what was off.

"I do order out too much," Mister Lewis replied, his fingertips probing for his silver chain.

The driver paused, face contorting to a sour expression.

"OK, you're right," Mister Lewis said in a conspiratorial voice. "You caught me. It's a trap."

Mister Lewis brought his arm up and snapped his wrist, lashing the delivery driver across the face with the silver chain. The chain left a smoking divot across the driver's cheek and the driver staggered backwards two steps, only to come to an abrupt halt.

"What the hell?" muttered the delivery driver, noticing the semi-circle of banded dollar bill stacks and not being happy about it.

As the driver glanced around wildly, The Investor tossed down more stacks of bills, starting to fill in the rest of the circle. The driver charged The Investor but came to a violent and sudden stop when confronted with the stack of bills on the ground between them. The driver clawed at the air in the direction of The Investor but couldn't seem to extend an arm over the stack of bills. Mister Lewis gave the driver another lash with the chain as The Investor threw down the last three stacks to close the circle.

"What kind of cult are you people?" sputtered the delivery driver, who turned slowly counterclockwise in a circle, staring in horror at the stacks of bills. "Have you raised the ghost of Marcus Crassus to torment me?"

"Well, no," Mister Lewis chuckled. "If I remember right, Marcus Crassus was into real estate and silver. My associate here is fonder of paper currency and apps."

"Crassus also trafficked in slaves," replied the delivery driver. "Are your apps so different from the slave pits?"

"I will not have you insulting the gig economy," shrieked The Investor.

"Don't take the bait," interrupted Mister Lewis, putting himself between The Investor and the delivery driver. "However, now that you mention apps, we really ought to have a chat about that app you followed here."

"Why would I ever want to talk to you about anything?" asked the delivery driver.

Mister Lewis smiled widely, then walked over to the window and parted the curtains, revealing a bay window.

"I'm not in a particular rush," said Mister Lewis. "I can wait until morning. All morning, in fact. My next appointment isn't until noon. Are you a morning person?"

"You have no intention of letting me walk out of here, regardless of whether I talk to you," the delivery driver stared daggers. "I am well aware of your ilk's... how do you so politely phrase it... 'containment protocols' for my kind."

"I'm sorry if I gave that impression," said Mister Lewis. "Yes, it's against protocol to let apex predators roam freely... and I do recall you trying to eat me. We both know that the plague metaphor fits the vector for how vampirism spreads. You're going to have to go. The question is how you go? It doesn't have to be as painful as the morning sun. Talk to me about how you crossed that threshold uninvited and where I can find whoever put you up to this."

"Obviously, I was invited," the delivery driver's eyes rolled.

"Delivery apps don't constitute a formal invitation," snapped Mister Lewis.

"I'm sorry," the delivery driver feigned sympathy. "I didn't realize I was speaking with an expert on the intersection of technology and the old ways. I wasn't invited, as you say, and yet... here I am. Ah, the wonders of technology. So many invitations and so few hours of moonlight."

"That's preposterous. There's no chain of intent. You weren't invited into the system. You weren't personally invited in."

The delivery driver merely smiled in reply.

"Technically," began The Investor, "that might not be accurate. One of the ways the app recruits delivery drivers is by having registered users invite their friends to be both users and drivers. We pay them a fee when someone signs up for either and it's even called an invitation. I mean, we romanticize the hiring process like that on purpose, but it's accurate to say you're invited when you're hired. And if I remember correctly, the deliveries are assigned to individual drivers instead of going into a pool, ergo a request to deliver the food. Does a request like that equate to an invitation in your world?"

The vampire frowned.

"I see," said Mister Lewis before turning his head towards The Investor. "Well, if the causal chain is that obvious, I guess I can take things from here. Isn't it customary to tip the driver?"

The Investor nodded and produced a stack of bills, then tossed it at the driver. It struck the driver just below the neck and melted its way straight through, decapitating the driver in the process.

"You were right about continual improvement," beamed The Investor. "This time we spent less on food before finding a vampire, acquired more information and decapitation is a more efficient way of disposing of a vampire, isn't it?"

Mister Lewis shook his head wearily as he stepped into the circle of money and picked up the delivery driver's smartphone. The Food Fling app was still displayed on it. He tapped on the account screen and scrolled until the employee number was visible before handing the phone to The Investor.

"I assume it's not hard to look up whoever referred this driver into the system?" he asked.

"Not a problem," replied The Investor.

"You do that while I properly dispose of these remains," said Mister Lewis. "I'm going to need an address for whoever did the referring on this driver and then the addresses of everyone else that was referred by that account. I'm going to purge the nest of the drones like this one and then I'm going to have a little visit with their master."

"I want to be there for their master," said The Investor.

"That's not a good idea," said Mister Lewis. "Your faith in money may be strong enough to take out the flunkies, but you're not trained and master vampires get that old by being hard to destroy. If you didn't take out a master on the first strike, you wouldn't live long enough for a second. Especially if you only damaged it and pissed it off. And that's before we get to the mesmerism problem. There are a lot of things that could go wrong, so it's safer if I'm not physically looking out for you while I handle this. Let me do what you pay me for."

7. A Returned Delivery

Mister Lewis approached the house. It was old, big and not particularly well lit with a long walkway between the front door and sidewalk. Basically, a house conforming to stereotypes for a monster's lair.

The lighting didn't get any better down the walkway or up the front steps. The front door was in shadow and presented the options of a doorbell or a large brass knocker. Mister Lewis opted for the knocker. Why fight the expectations when so much trouble has been taken to set them? Besides, if the doorbell sounded like a buzzard with tuberculosis, it would be too much and spoil the mood.

He waited and the door eventually opened.

"Food delivery," said Mister Lewis, holding up a cell phone with the Food Fling app on it.

"Yes, I suppose I am hungry," said The Master of the House. "Enter."

The Master of the House stepped to the side and Mister Lewis entered. He was careful to enter sideways and continue to face his host, lest his back be exposed.

"I assume you'll want to talk before I dine," said The Master of the House while closing the door behind Mister Lewis.

"I'm that obvious?" asked Mister Lewis.

"I'm a little older than what you've probably been encountering," said The Master of the House with a patronizing smile. "If you're... experienced enough, people with a strong sense of belief look a little different. People who have weaponized their belief system look even more different to the trained eye. Let's just say that I appreciate your tan. Very George Hamilton, although I believe Hamilton was on my team, not yours."

"You're not the first person to tell me something like that tonight," Mister Lewis returned the smile.

"That seemed likely," conceded The Master of the House. "You're so 'tan,' I'm not sure one of my children would be able to partake of you. Particularly the younger ones. Fear not, I have a much stronger stomach."

"I figured you'd feel that way," said Mister Lewis, reaching his hand inside his jacket.

Suddenly, The Master of the House was on him, hand around his throat.

"Slowly," whispered The Master of the House. "You wouldn't happen to have a crucifix in your pocket, would you? We don't need any of that. By the looks of you, you could do a bit of damage if you started focusing all that prodigious belief on some religious iconography."

Mister Lewis slowly removed his hand from his jacket, producing a single piece of paper from an inner pocket.

"No crucifix," said Mister Lewis. "Just a list. Nothing holy about this list either. I just wanted to talk to you about how you came to invite your nest to be delivery drivers for a food delivery app."

"I believe they call it 'referring a friend' in the app," The Master of the House returned to the smarmy grin.

"Oh, I think we'd both call it something else," said Mister Lewis. "But it's very odd how your nest was freely crossing thresholds when they made those deliveries. It suggests a chain of consent. I'll ask again. How did you come to invite your nest to Food Fling?"

"Of course, there was a chain of consent," laughed The Master of the House. "I received an invitation to the app. A very presumptuous thing it is, too. So many permissions given so freely. Truly, that invitation was a gift. I was also given some... suggestions... regarding how my nest might find the app useful and how to share that gift. It was working, too. What is that colloquialism? A brother has to eat?"

"Who invited you into the app?"

"I think I get a question now," The Master of the House's smile faded. "Am I to understand I'm the last name on your list that you've visited?"

"That's correct," replied Mister Lewis.

"Then my nest is no more?"

"That's also correct. So, who invited you into the app?"

"No," said The Master of the House. "I think you only need to have one question answered. Especially if I have to rebuild a nest."

The Master of the House stared longingly into Mister Lewis's eyes and said, "won't you tell me who trained you to weaponize your faith?"

Mister Lewis stared back, first blankly, then bemusedly.

"You don't mesmerize," The Master of the House said in wonder. "Aren't you the rare bird?"

"That works better on people with low self-esteem," replied Mister Lewis. "You probably find a lot of that around here, though. Now where were we? I remember. We were talking about who invited you to the app."

"I think I shall invite myself to dine on you," the grip on Mister Lewis's throat tightened. "You did mention a food delivery and one of us shouldn't be rude this evening."

"Here's the thing," Mister Lewis held up his index finger. "You're missing the causal link."

"Link between what," growled The Master of the House.

"You can't mesmerize me because I have self-esteem, but I'm not carrying a crucifix."

"I fail to see a connection," The Master of the House's fangs were now exposed.

"The crucifix is for focusing your belief on an object of your faith. What happens when someone believes in themself?"

Mister Lewis dropped his index finger and raised his middle finger.

The Master of the House glanced at the middle finger. If jokes had been made about Mister Lewis having a tan, this was something else entirely. To the Master of the House's trained eyes, the 'tan' of someone who'd weaponized their belief had initially turned into a faint glow. Then it exploded like someone had lit phosphorus on fire. The Master of the House let go of his throat and stumbled backwards in shock and pain.

"You can believe in a lot of things," continued Mister Lewis. His finger still looked normal to his eyes, but he wasn't a vampire. "Not all of them require you to carry a symbol to focus on. I prefer being my own symbol."

The Master of the House had backed into a wall and retreated along it until hitting a corner. Mister Lewis followed, arm out and finger extended.

"Seriously," Mister Lewis glanced at his finger and back at The Master of the House. "I believe in everything my finger represents right now. Did you want to tell me who invited you?"

"No," hissed The Master of the House.

Mister Lewis tapped the point of his middle finger on the Master of the House's forehead twice, leaving a pair of smoking indentations.

"Find it yourself," The Master of the House growled before spitting in Mister Lewis's face.

"Fine. Have it your way."

Mister Lewis tapped the forehead again and pressed his finger through the skull, melting a hole around it. The body went slack and dropped. With his off hand, he grabbed the Master of the House's hair and pulled while his middle finger burnt through the neck. The head came free, and he tossed it to the other side of the room before exhaling audibly.

"So, somebody hates my client enough to invite a vampire lord to ruin his business," he muttered to himself. "That would be a lot easier to narrow down if he was more of a people person."

Mister Lewis looked at his hand, which coated with ichor and ooze, some of which was crispy and solid as though it had been fried. He wiped his hand clean on the body, lit a fire on the floor and left to contemplate a suspect list as the house began to burn itself clean.

Brain Dead

1. Brain Dead

While it might have felt like a witch's circle, it was really an app circle. Five teens were loosely arranged in a circle, playing the "Brain Dead" app, a mobile game based upon the "Famous for Being Famous" reality show that celebrated the power of money to enable carefree behavior and the empowerment to break with social norms. The teens were engrossed, imagining themselves embroiled in a world of questionable celebrity. It made for a quieter room than you'd normally find with five teens inhabiting it.

The quiet didn't last. One teen let out a pained grunt as a phone dropped to the floor. The teen grunted a second time, tried to stand up and then collapsed to the floor, lying on top of the phone.

It took a minute, but the rest of the circle eventually looked up from their phones and peered quizzically at the prone form on the ground.

As the circle contemplated responding, the teen awkwardly stood back up.

"Doghouses for fame," slurred the teen, head leaning to the right at an unusual angle. "Points for mirrors."

The circle exchanged puzzled glances.

"Death for fame," the teen continued to slur before attempting to take a step, failing and falling to one knee. "Fame for death. Death brings fame."

"Are you OK?" one of the circle finally found a voice.

"Venom spews fame," rasped the teen before face-planting.

"Should we call an ambulance?" asked another of the circle.

After their turn in the game was completed, one of them did.

2. Even Better Than Real Life

"**D**on't look at me," screamed The Reality Star. "Turn around and face the wall when in my presence."

Mister Lewis considered the source and didn't bother replying. The source was the "star" of the "Famous for Being Famous" reality show and that fame was attained by being a limited cognitive processer with difficulties recognizing social norms and boundaries. There were rumors that the reality show was really a performance that deliberately hid a cutthroat mastermind behind a smokescreen of stupidity. Mister Lewis contemplated that and decided cutthroat and dim didn't necessarily have to be mutually exclusive qualities in a person.

"He's okay," interjected The Investor, who was either not fazed by such antics or had grown accustomed to them.

"He's not the help?" The Reality Star seemed a different flavor of confused than in the show.

"Yes and no," offered The Investor. "He's not staff, if that's what you mean. He's more like a specialist I bring in when strange things like this start happening."

"I'm the guy who keeps you from getting eaten when the wolves knock down your door," Mister Lewis hoped his sunglasses concealed the rolling of his eyes. "Would someone mind telling me what kind of wolves are causing a fuss today?"

"One of my startups produces a mobile game based on the Famous for Being Famous show," explained The Investor. "The game is called Brain Dead."

Mister Lewis thought it would be best politically if he refrained from comment about the app's name. Sometimes feigning ignorance was safer.

"The game simulates the show by having the user act out," continued The Investor.

"Excuse me," The Reality Star spoke over The Investor. "Performing acts of social daring and growing your fame by acquiring media coverage in a simulated world. My brand is aspirational for the 16-24 demographic and we will stick to the brand."

"Correct, as always," The Investor nodded gravely. "The problem is we're starting to see some... medical incidents among game users. Users are collapsing while playing the game. Babbling incoherently and then collapsing. Some of them are in a coma. The ones who regain consciousness don't seem to be responsive. They're just... babbling."

"Are we talking speaking in tongues?" asked Mister Lewis.

"I don't think so," answered The Investor. "It would depend on what you mean by 'tongues.' They aren't speaking a foreign language, more like random phrases strung together. Like a toddler repeating words without knowing what they mean. Given... what's been going on... this seems like something you should look into before we commit to a promotional strategy."

"This isn't flashing lights from the game causing epileptic seizures?" asked Mister Lewis.

"That's been ruled out, medically," replied The Investor.

"Given the... nature of previous problems," Mister Lewis hesitated to speak of the undead around The Reality Star. "Have any of these game users died?"

"Not that we've heard of," replied The Investor. "But some of them are in comas, so that might not last. The doctors seem to be confused. It's not clear that the medical community is aware of the scope of this yet. The complaints we're getting are from the families of users, not the Centers for Disease Control. Ideally, you can clean this up or confirm it's a natural medical phenomenon before the CDC catches on. We'd really like to be ahead of the CDC with our promotion."

"What we've previously been dealing with has revolved around people dying," Mister Lewis chose his words carefully. "If everyone is surviving these incidents, it lowers the odds this is my kind of problem. How are you planning to promote this app if it turns out to be a series of random accidents?"

"We seize the opportunity to trumpet how our app amazes and delights," The Reality Star had conviction, if nothing else. "When our users collapse and are incoherent after playing the game, it just shows how powerful the game is. 'Scientifically proven to blow your mind' will be the new slogan. My demographic wants to have their mind blown. If we're lucky, we can have a forbidden fruit feel to it. That would drive downloads through the roof. Ideally, we'd be able to tie 'blow your mind' to my old sex video, but too many of the game users are under 18 and we don't want to get download restrictions on the app, so we can probably only imply that a little."

Mister Lewis again chose to say nothing.

"Your usual fee?" The Investor sought confirmation.

"My usual fee," Mister Lewis nodded. "Are any of the victims local? I'm going to need to see this for myself."

3. The Blown Mind

The teen was strapped into a hospital bed. The straps held the arms and legs in place, but not the neck. The neck could still move, and the teen's head flopped around like a fish on dry land trying to get back into the water.

"Free trade fame," the teen's tone was a moan, but the volume was a yell. "Ice cream pepper celebration."

Mister Lewis stood in the hallway peering into the teen's hospital room. He produced a monocle from his pocket, raised it to his eye and frowned.

"Can I help you?" asked a doctor who was walking by.

"Isn't that a little slow for the amount of thrashing?" asked Mister Lewis, gesturing at the heart monitor and its slow blips.

"It's an unusual case," said the doctor. "Yes, the vitals are low... but there doesn't appear to be any of the lethargy or loss of strength you'd expect to see with that."

"What's the patient saying?" continued Mister Lewis. "I'm not really understanding the meaning of anything I'm hearing. Should I be? Is there a previous conversation that gives it context or is it some kind of manic behavior? Perhaps hypomanic?"

"Certainly not hypomanic," the doctor gave Mister Lewis a closer look. "The volume when speaking and the movement would be full blown manic, but that kind of an episode still wouldn't explain the low vitals. But no, what the patient has been saying doesn't make any sense to us, either. In the emergency room, we thought it might be hysteria, but the sedatives had no effect."

"Sedatives with that slow a heartbeat?" asked Mister Lewis.

"It wasn't that slow on arrival," the doctor quickly straightened up. "It's been gradually slowing, and the sedatives have been out of the system for some time. Are you an attorney? Did the family send you?"

"Let's just say I'm observing," Mister Lewis brought the monocle back up to his eye. "Probably should have been here a little earlier. Still, it looks like I'm in time for the change and that could be the most important thing to observe going forward. Brace yourself. This is about to get weirder."

"Change?" the doctor's voice went up an octave. "I think you'd better leave."

"Wait for it," Mister Lewis raised a finger. "And... now."

The teen convulsed, almost jumping out of the restraints, and then suddenly was still. The eyes were open and empty. The heart monitor flatlined.

"You need to leave," the doctor shoved Mister Lewis aside and ran into the room.

A crash cart followed.

As the doctor raised the defibrillator paddles, sure enough, it got weirder.

"Reality dogs rollerblades," said the teen, eyes still empty.

The doctor's eye's shot to the heart monitor, which was still flatlined.

The doctor set down the paddles and examined the heart monitor patches on the teen's chest. All appeared to be in order.

"Garden pliers boxes," said the teen.

The doctor felt for the carotid artery, frowned, then grabbed the teen's wrist.

"There's no pulse," stammered the doctor.

"Phone loin fame," said the teen in a louder voice.

"You might want to back up," called Mister Lewis from the hallway.

As the doctor started to form a word in reply, the teen sat straight up, ripping the restraints off the bed in doing so.

"Mirror gravel ant," said the teen, who turned sideways to get out of bed. Still grasping the teen's wrist in search of a pulse, the doctor got pulled along for the ride.

"You need to rest," the doctor tried to force the teen back into bed.

The teen swung an arm, and the doctor went crashing into the nurses who'd responded to the flatline.

Mister Lewis stepped back and watched the teen slowly stagger out the door and turn right down the hallway.

"The patient's heart stopped," the doctor had reached the doorway.

"That's correct," Mister Lewis stuck out an arm to stop the doctor. "And it's still stopped."

"We have to get," began the doctor.

"You have a deceased patient walking out of the hospital," interrupted Mister Lewis. "You're having a little trouble processing it, but you know what you saw. You need to give the patient a little room or someone's likely to get hurt. I'm not sure if your patient is likely to pass that condition on through bites or not."

"You know what's going on?" asked the doctor.

"Not completely," answered Mister Lewis. "But when the dead get up and walk away, there's generally someone telling them to. Let your patient walk away. I'm going to follow your patient and at the end of our walk, I'm likely to get a better idea of who's giving the marching orders here or at least what they want. This is out of your hands now."

"What do we tell the family?" asked the doctor.

"The patient left without checking out," offered Mister Lewis. "Nobody's likely to believe what you've seen. The more you talk about it, the more questions the lawyers are going to ask. Could be licensing issues. Your malpractice insurance will go up, guaranteed. If you stop and think about it, you probably didn't see anything. Hell, you probably never talked to me, either."

"No," whispered the doctor. "I don't suppose I did."

The teen had made it to the end of the hall and shambled around the corner. Mister Lewis leisurely strolled behind, wondering where the trip would end.

4. Popular with the Dead

T wenty minutes later, Mister Lewis was still following the dead teen down an increasingly congested
sidewalk when his cell phone rang. The Investor's name
flashed across the screen and after a moment's internal
debate, he answered it.

"I have news," said Mister Lewis into the phone. "We
have more zombies."

"What?" The Investor's near- shriek came through
the speaker partially digitized. "That's the last thing we
need."

"That Brain Dead victim you sent me to check on
is dead," said Mister Lewis. "We're both having a nice
walk now. I've been tailing our newly deceased friend
for about half a mile. I might know a little bit more when
we get to wherever we're going."

"That can wait," said the Investor. "Our friend, The
Reality Star, has a problem over at the Bigly Mall. There
was supposed to be some kind of personal appearance
and the crowd's getting really ugly. Can you get over
there and see if it's related?"

"That's in the direction we're walking in," replied Mister Lewis. "It very well might be related. Are we talking
a crowd of people or a crowd of zombies?"

"Teenagers, as far as I know," said The Investor.

"I'm following a teenage zombie right now," said Mister Lewis. "We'll either be turning into the mall or passing by in a couple blocks. I'll call you back when I know more."

The dead teen turned a corner and was now headed in a straight line towards Bigly Mall. Since it was a bit too much of a coincidence, Mister Lewis jogged ahead and immediately noticed more vaguely teenaged people heading towards the mall entrance with a similar unsteady stagger to the dead teen.

Upon entering, it was easy to follow the din of the cacophony to an open space in the mall's center. The Reality Star was on a stage, nervously chattering away, while a crowd was slowly being pushed out of the way by staggering teens with their heads at odd angles, chattering away at unseen conversational partners and not making just a ton of sense. While the living audience was clearly disturbed and a portion of them were starting to bolt, no one seemed to know quite what to make of the interlopers.

Mister Lewis circled around to the back of the stage and climbed its stairs. The Reality Star was too busy attempting to chat up an upcoming album – while scanning the crowd with increasing concern – to notice his approach.

"Time to go," said Mister Lewis after placing a hand over the microphone.

The Reality Star opened a mouth to protest, but Mister Lewis grabbed an arm and pulled.

"Do not engage with anyone," said Mister Lewis. "Do not stop. Do not let anyone close their fingers around you. We are headed towards those stairs. Now follow."

The two weaved their way through the crowd. Teeth chattered in their direction, empty eyes stared, and arms pawed, but they were able to make the stairs with a minimum of physical contact. Half a flight up, Mister Lewis stopped to survey the room.

"You seem popular," Mister Lewis began the left-handed compliment. "It looks like they're following you and you've got fans dying to meet you."

"That's how it works when you're famous," sniffed The Reality Star.

"I meant that a little more literally," said Mister Lewis. "You see how most of their heads are at strange angles and flopping around?"

"Yes?"

"That's because they're not alive. Those fans are re-animated."

"Bullshit. They look alive to me."

"No, they're just freshly dead. They haven't started to decompose yet. Look at the movements, not the skin. I also witnessed one of them reanimating. That's what led me here."

The Reality Star scanned the crowd, eyes widening.

"Is being chased by zombies good publicity?" The Reality Star accidentally said out loud.

"Oh, that would be news," replied Mister Lewis. "But you'll come off as crazy and needy if you're the first one to say it. With any luck, I'll have this shut down before it gets that far. To an outside observer, this will look like a disaffected teen fan base acting out. Nothing out of the ordinary. Unless you know what you're looking for, you'd assume they're alive. The real problem is that they seem to be tracking you. The one I followed here came directly from the hospital after dying. In damn near a straight line, too. First things, first... we need to get you out of here."

"Are they here to eat my brains or something?" asked The Reality Star.

"That's certainly possible," said Mister Lewis. "But it's probably best we don't stick around and find out exactly what they're supposed to do when they find you. It's also best if we leave before they're packed in more tightly. They don't seem particularly coordinated, even for zombies, although that could be because they're fresh. Let's not wait around to see if their movements start looking orchestrated. We're going up the stairs and out the back, just the way we left the stage."

So, they went up the stairs and wound through the crowds. Mister Lewis was mostly left alone, but the undead fan base reached out and occasionally brushed The Reality Star's limbs and torso as they rushed by. The Reality Star could not help but notice the occasional chomping of teeth in their general direction and couldn't decide whether the dead were hungry, or it was more personal.

"You need to get far away from here," said Mister Lewis as they reached the street.

"You want me to drive north or something?" asked The Reality Star.

"Where is that Brain Dead app popular, geographically?" asked Mister Lewis.

"Everywhere."

"Then you're likely to run into more of them if you drive north. Do you have access to a boat?"

"Duh," The Reality Star's eyes rolled. "It's part of the brand."

"Then get to that boat and head at least a mile off-shore and wait. The dead seldom swim, and this lot doesn't look coordinated enough to try. It should go without saying, nobody on the boat with you should get anywhere near that gaming app until we know exactly what's going on. Wait for a phone call for the all clear or instructions on what to do next. Can you do that?"

The Reality Star nodded and hailed a taxi. As the taxi drove away, Mister Lewis turned back towards the mall. The reanimated fans were starting to emerge and slowly lumbered in the same direction the taxi had taken.

5. The Gamification of Death

"Why didn't you just kill them?" moaned The Investor. "I've seen what you can do to vampires. Vampires are more dangerous than zombies, aren't they?"

"It's more complicated than that," replied Mister Lewis. "My... background makes it a lot easier for me to deal with vampires than most people. Especially if they don't know I'm coming. Yes, in a one-on-one situation, vampires are usually more dangerous than zombies. Zombies aren't really that bad if you only run into one. The trouble with zombies is they tend to show up in large numbers and you can't effectively fight a mob hand-to-hand. The zombies were swarming and that was going to be an insurmountable problem quickly if we didn't get out of there immediately.

"In terms of fighting zombies, there's not much you can do in a situation like that except maybe try to light them on fire and see how many of them you could burn. Of course, then you'd likely end up burning down that mall and who knows how many of the surrounding buildings. And then you'd have a lawsuit over property damages. And since those corpses were so fresh, you'd have trouble convincing their families they were already deceased before you lit them on fire, so there would be wrongful death suits, likely some murder charges. Really, that's a lot of bad publicity you don't want."

"Fine, it was a no-win situation," sighed The Investor. "But I've got a high-profile licensing partner stuck on a yacht with a crowd gathering on shore. Should anything happen to that partner, I lose money. If the gaming app gets hit with some health scare, I lose money and maybe the whole gaming company. The only upside I'm seeing is a tax write-off if the company folds. Am I being targeted again?"

"Too early to tell," said Mister Lewis, fishing his monocle out of his pocket. "This monocle is a sort of filter. It lets you see certain types of magical activity. When I got to the hospital, that teen you sent me to have a look at had something mystical happening inside the skull. It was growing and it was pretty clear whatever it was, was about to pop. When it popped, the teen died and almost immediately reanimated to go looking for The Reality Star. The question is which one of you is being targeted? Either way, those fresh corpses are a genius way to box you in."

"It's those necromancers," The Investor shivered. "They're back, aren't they?"

"Could be," replied Mister Lewis. "This is closer to their M.O. I think it's time I had a look at this 'Brain Dead' app before anything else happens."

"It'll be on the second screen of apps," said The Investor, handing Mister Lewis a mobile phone.

Mister Lewis swiped to the second screen and tapped on the Brain Dead icon. The game loaded.

"You said the object of this game is to get famous," Mister Lewis frowned at the screen. "How do you make money off this?"

"Two ways," said The Investor. "There's some income for ads displayed during the game, but the real profit engine is in-app purchases."

"Which means?" Mister Lewis tapped the screen again.

"Players spend money to buy things inside the game. Items to help them level up faster. Customized avatars to make their characters look more like them. That sort of thing."

"So, you make money by people paying to take short-cuts to fame in a game about fame?"

"Absolutely," The Investor laughed. "And the target audience is eager to shell out for it. A lot of games make more money off advertising, but not this one. Don't underestimate the vanity appeal of a lookalike avatar. That reality show draws in a wonderfully dedicated and lucrative audience."

"And by dedicated, you mean gullible?"

"If only P.T. Barnum were alive now. He'd know what to do with the demographic targeting tools these apps afford us."

"So, if I tap here, I buy... a fan club... and that levels me up?"

"It raises your Q Score and the number of followers. Then the combination of those two components levels you up, but yes."

Mister Lewis tapped the screen to buy a fan club and suddenly his brain felt like it was on fire. He screamed in pain and through the phone against the wall. The pain subsided a little as he brought is foot down on the phone and stomped on it. The sound of the LCD screen cracking was a small release.

"Those things are expensive," shouted The Investor.

"Your app tried to bite me," growled Mister Lewis. "That hurt."

"Wait," The Investor raised an eyebrow. "Are you saying my app is magic?"

"Probably cursed, if you want to be technical about it," replied Mister Lewis. "This isn't my first rodeo and that still hurt. It confirms where these zombies are coming from, though."

"Are you saying the game is killing its users?"

"That might be oversimplifying it, but close enough. If this wasn't an active situation, I'd want to do a little more testing to confirm it, but it looks like when someone tries to make a purchase, the purchase triggers an attack on the brain. Might be buying a fan club, might be buying anything. The exact trigger probably doesn't matter at this point, but the effects of that attack are what's ultimately causing all this death and reanimation. You need to shut down the servers."

"Wait," The Investor's jaw was slack. "Are you saying my servers are cursed, too?"

"Unclear. Depends on exactly how the purchase is triggered. But even if it's just the app, you don't want any more downloads until this is sorted out and you want as much offline as possible. Pull it from app platforms, too."

"But the instillation vector is one of the things that establishes value when selling the game company," The Investor reddened.

"Spin it like that Flappy Bird game," Mister Lewis offered. "It's now a limited edition and a rare prize. Come back with an updated version when we've contained this situation. It sounds like your audience would eat that up. Besides, if this gets publicly linked to the game, more downloads mean more liability."

The Investor went from red to ashen in a shockingly short period of time.

"You're sure these zombies can't swim?" asked the Investor.

"Reasonably sure. Why?"

The investor turned a computer monitor around and pointed. A gossip website had pictures of a crowd gathering at the marina, touting it as The Reality Star fleeing a loyal fan base.

"That headline's not entirely wrong," sighed Mister Lewis. "Not unexpected, either. Look, you get those servers taken down and remove the app from the online stores. I'll go see if anyone's learned to swim and maybe I can glean something from the crowd about where this came from."

"Publicity," murmured The Investor. "Unruly fans are still good publicity. Please don't light them on fire on camera?"

6. Dead Droppings

The scene at the marina was consistent with the gossip site's account of it. The reanimated fans, Mister Lewis guessed they were in their mid-teens through early 20s, were lining up along the waterfront of the marina. They weren't standing still, more like shuffling in place, flapping their arms and speaking the incoherent babble that was a hallmark of the outbreak. It was loud and it was starting to get crowded as a steady trickle of reanimated newcomers staggered up to join the scene.

That the reanimated fans hadn't jumped into the water was interesting. Were they closely controlled drones that hadn't been ordered to yet? Was there a vestigial sense of their limitations left from their unorthodox creation? Would they effectively gain a little courage and start stepping off the pier as they stalked their target?

It was hard to say. It was also hard to say how long they could stay out in the hot sun before the decay became more apparent. Particularly the scent of rot. There were a lot of ways this could go wrong.

Mister Lewis noticed the shadow falling over him an instant before he felt the splatter on his shoulder. He glanced down. Bird droppings. Bird droppings streaked with blood?

He looked up at the source of the shadow. As you would expect at a marina, it was a sea gull. A partially decomposed seagull with a rotted, featherless face.

The gull glided down and landed on a bench.

"Our paths cross once more," said the gull in a raspy voice. "We thought we might find a familiar face here."

"We wiped the servers," an edge slipped into Mister Lewis's voice. "The website is no more. The app is no more. They've both been taken down. You don't need to be doing this."

"And what precisely do you think we're doing?" rasped the gull.

"Someone's doing a large-scale reanimation," Mister Lewis gestured towards the crowd. "You've already moved on one of my client's properties. You want me to believe this is a coincidence?"

The gull laughed and then spat out blood flecked with tiny pieces of its disintegrating lungs.

"No," rasped the gull. "We have no belief in coincidence, either. You were helpful before, we thought you might be helpful again. You seem to understand the gravity of such things and have incentive to restore balance."

"What kind of help are you looking for?"

"Information. Information on how this came to start. From whom it came to start. But you seem unaware as to who started it."

"It appears someone ensorcelled an app," began Mister Lewis. "A video game on mobile phones."

"Yes, we know what an app is. We do not live in the dark ages."

"My apologies," continued Mister Lewis. "It appears when the user plays the game, possibly when they try to purchase something in the game, they are attacked. At first glance, some sort of spell or curse affecting the brain. I arrived to witness the spell killing one of these kids. It took a few hours, but the victim died and was reanimated. Just got up and immediately shambled off in the direction of The Reality Star the game was based on. I sent The Reality Star to get on a boat and get offshore, out of reach. That's why there's a crowd here. They're waiting for the boat. One of my client's companies made the game. That's as much as I know right now."

"This is consistent with our findings," rasped the gull. "It is an old curse, similar to some of what was put on that website you so graciously dismantled. Or rather a variation on it. Someone wished not to be seen by us. Someone attempted to lighten the spell. To merely damage the brain, kill the thought processes and leave the body alive. A brain-dead body commanded like a zombie, but not technically reanimated. The spell was a partial failure. The culprit has acquired their bodies, but they are dead bodies, and we could not help but notice so many things being reanimated. We do not condone such public displays."

"Your semi-competent sorcerer has a sick sense of humor," said Mister Lewis.

"How is that?"

"The name of the gaming app is Brain Dead."

The gull laughed again, louder.

"How very literal," rasped the gull.

"Does this mean you have no interest in my client?" asked Mister Lewis.

"It would be premature to say such a thing. We have yet to determine the nature of the relationship between our wayward dabbler in the realm of the dead and your client."

A loud splash caused both Mister Lewis and the gull to turn towards the marina. The first zombie had fallen into the water.

"It won't be long before more of them stumble into the drink," said Mister Lewis. "I don't think either of us wants attention drawn to this. Can you de-animate those bodies?"

"We think it would be better if you did that yourself," rasped the gull. "Go to the place where we first spoke."

"The Founder's backyard?"

"You will find what you seek there."

"And that's why you think my client's involved?"

"Oh, there is a relationship. Be certain of that. Perhaps you can find the perpetrator of this failed curse before we do. Identify the sorcerer and all will be forgiven. If you cannot take the sorcerer alive, well... it would not be the first time we raised the dead for punishment. If you cannot identify the sorcerer... we shall see how the cards fall."

With that, the gull flapped its wings and took to the sky. It left feathers behind where it had been sitting.

Another splash brought Mister Lewis back to reality. It wasn't going to be much longer before someone tried to pull one of the reanimated bodies from the water.

7. The Mobile Phone Fetish

The police tape had come and gone from The Founder's backyard. Mister Lewis entered it much the way he had before. The grass wasn't quite recovered from the police forensic team trampling it, but it was mostly the same as he'd originally found it.

Where the remnants of The Founder's body had laid after the zombie ants had partially devoured him, Mister Lewis found a mobile phone. The phone must've had its screensaver deactivated. It was hot enough to have been running for hours and the Brain Dead app shown on its screen. Bound to the phone with a rawhide strap was a crude wooden carving of a man.

A barbeque grill stood a few feet from the phone. Mister Lewis opened the grill, removed the grate, turned the gas on high and lit it. He then went to a tree and snapped off a foot's length of branch. He snagged the phone by the rawhide strap with the branch, carried it over to the barbeque and dropped it in. The carving smoldered for a moment and caught fire.

Mister Lewis closed the lid and pulled his cell phone out of a pocket.

"Something's happening at the marina," The Investor's voice spouted forth after half a ring.

"Let me guess," replied Mister Lewis. "The crowd is collapsing?"

"Sort of. They were all in the water, but now they're just floating and not moving. All kinds of ambulances being called."

"That's probably better for you. The medical examiner will be confused by the time of death and the lungs won't look like drowning, but everyone will have been seen jumping in. They'll do tox screens. Those will come back negative. They'll either write it off has a lab error or decide the crowd fell victim to some kind of mass hysteria. They'll want to move on."

"Was it you stopping it?"

"Yes, and you're not going to like it. I found a cell phone running the app with a fetish tied to it in The Founder's backyard. It was exactly where I left The Founder's Body. That's where the curse sprang forth from. I'm burning it."

"Why was it there?"

"Somebody's sending a message. They either want you to know why this is happening or they want you to know who did it and they're being too clever about it. That's not the worst thing I've discovered, either. The Necromancers are back. They're the ones who told me where to find the phone. They insist there's a relationship between you and whoever did this and they'd like to know what it is. Based on the scene here, I'd have to agree with them. Someone's out to get you and they're willing to make a very public display to do so."

The Investor did not reply.

The Wisdom of the Deceased

1. Strange Visitor From Another Grave

The Investor was in the outer office when Mister Lewis answered the summons. That was a little unusual, in and of itself, but the crashing noises from The Investor's private office were stranger still.

"He's trashing my office," groaned the Investor. "You have to make him go away."

"Who's trashing your office?" asked Mister Lewis.

"Tom Tasker."

"Tom Tasker? Computer guy? Always in a black turtleneck?"

"The savior of personal computing. Yes, that's him."

"I thought he died?"

"Of course," said the Investor, gesturing towards the office door. "That's why I called you. If he were alive, I'd just have called security."

Mister Lewis opened the door a crack and peeked in. Sure enough, there was the upper torso of Tom Tasker, complete with trademark turtleneck, floating above The Investor's desk. Tasker would wave his arm and objects would fly across the room. When a checkbook struck the doorframe, Tasker noticed he had an audience.

"You bungler," screamed Tasker. "Why do you have a job? There is no aesthetic in this office! You're done in this industry!"

"Aaaaaand he's even a screamer in death," said Mister Lewis as he closed the door.

"He was a different person outside the office," offered The Investor. "Everyone swears he was a sweetheart."

"I think you've got Office Tom," replied Mister Lewis. "With everything flying around, this falls broadly under the category of Poltergeist activity. When and how did he first manifest?"

"It was about 2 hours ago when the app summoned him."

"What app?"

"I was being pitched a new startup," said The Investor.

2. The Digital Séance

"The app is called Wisdom of the Deceased," The Investor paused to take a deep breath. "They were pitching it to me as Cameo, but for the dead. Instead of having a celebrity leave you a video message, this app would let the user summon up someone who's deceased and ask them for advice."

"How does that even," Mister Lewis paused and shook his head. "Never mind. It's another cursed app. Did you ask for Tasker or was he suggested to you?"

"Are you kidding? Tom Tasker has created more value than just about anyone! His advice would be invaluable. Except... he won't stop yelling. Or throwing things around the room."

"And the people pitching the app?"

"They left the building shortly after we fled my office. Don't get me wrong. As far as app demos go, this is one of the more interesting ones. Not everything works in the beta version, but it's compelling as a work in progress. It might be worth making a small investment in on the chance they can bring it under control."

"Lovely," Mister Lewis's frown deepened. "An app for conducting séances. Did anyone draw or form a circle before summoning the spirit?"

"No. I just pressed a button and said his name."

"Uncontained," Mister Lewis winced. "I suppose it could be worse. You didn't summon anyone that was actually homicidal, just a spirit with anger issues. This might be a tricky one. Normally, you conduct an exorcism with the ceremony used by the deceased's religion. That doesn't really work with someone who worshipped themself."

"Isn't that how you got rid of the vampires?"

"No. There's a subtle difference between having faith in yourself and worshipping yourself. Come along, I may need to borrow some of your gear."

The Investor nodded, somewhat reluctantly, and they re-entered the office.

"Incompetents," screamed the spirit of Tom Tasker in what passed for a greeting. "Where is your work ethic?"

"Glad to see you're keeping the struggle alive," Mister Lewis replied to the spirit. "I was just remarking to my colleague here 'Don't let perfect be the enemy of good.' I believe it was Voltaire who said that?"

"How dare you," screamed the spirit of Tasker. "You will never escape mediocrity. Why are you still here? Pack your desk up and leave. I banish you!"

"So, Tom," Mister Lewis smiled and produced his cell phone. "You like my new phone? It's an Android."

The spirit hissed, pointed and a book flew off a shelf and almost knocked the phone out of Mister Lewis's hand.

"You remember your Shakespeare?" Mister Lewis asked the spirit. "King Lear? 'Striving to better, oft we mar what's well.' Why that's as applicable today as it was in the 1600s."

"You have perfection, or you have nothing," screamed the spirit. "Your services are no longer required!"

"Is your tablet still in the top drawer of the desk?" Mister Lewis asked The Investor.

The Investor nodded, so Mister Lewis approached the desk and stared the spirit of Tom Tasker in the eyes as he reached into the desk drawer and pulled out the digital tablet.

"You're familiar with this?" Mister Lewis asked the spirit as he held up the tablet.

"That is perfection," came the reply.

"No," said Mister Lewis. "It got much, much better. Observe."

Mister Lewis stuck his hand back into the drawer and pulled out a stylus. He clicked on an icon and proceeded to write "THIS IS PROGRESS" on the tablet's screen.

"Now I can write on the tablet," Mister Lewis said, holding the tablet up for the spirit to read.

"Blasphemy," screamed the spirit. The spirit's head was now shimmering. "I expressly forbid that. How dare they desecrate my beautiful tablet!?!"

"The users loved it," a smirk slid across Mister Lewis's face. "The board loved it. I think your replacement loved it most of all."

The spirit of Tom Tasker opened his mouth to scream and then exploded before a sound could come out.

"Did you just exorcise a ghost by antagonizing him?" asked The Investor.

"Sometimes you can dispel a ghost by making it realize it's dead," explained Mister Lewis. "Your hero sounded like he was the same autocratic control freak in death as in life, so I contradicted his methods and suggested his former underlings had moved on without him. I'm not sure if I exorcised him or he decided to go haunt his former company. I suspect there are some people who'd be happy if he did."

"And some people would say he's already been doing that," said The Investor.

3. The Startup Family

"Explain to me about the app that did this," said Mister Lewis. "Was it summoning spirits on purpose or was this some multimedia app with inspirational quotes that spit out an angry ghost instead of an archive video?"

"Oh, no," explained The Investor. "This was expressly about communication with the dead. I could make a lot of money with that kind of an offering. It's a service that's not been properly commercialized for mass consumption and we could have a first mover advantage if we move quickly."

"You didn't find the timing a little odd?" Mister Lewis rubbed at his temples. "All this trouble you've been having with paranormal issues and somebody chooses now to show up with a magical app? The question is whether they were on the level and just weren't competent at constructing the spell or were they hoping the spirit would kill you and they failed in that mission? Either way, we're looking at a real problem."

"But I know them," squeaked The Investor. "They've worked for me before."

"Who are they?"

"They were early hires for that urban dictionary app."

"The one you originally brought me in to investigate?"

"That's right."

"The one where The Founder was executed for posting necromantic spells online?"

"That's how you characterized his death. I wasn't there."

"The one where the same necromancers who executed The Founder were making veiled threats towards me and especially towards you if those spells weren't scrubbed from online and the whole mess cleaned up?"

"Well, that was the other reason I called you here."

"Give me the address," whispered Mister Lewis. "Maybe they haven't attracted undue attention, but I have a bad feeling I know what they used to build that app. Whether it's intentional or not, they could get all of us killed if they're using the necromantic postings from that app."

4. The Scientific Method

The would-be séance app's offices were in a run-down one-story building that had somehow escaped gentrification. The labels on the buzzer at the building's entrance indicated three companies were housed within. The buzzer did not seem to work. Fortunately, neither did the lock on the front door.

Mister Lewis entered the building and noted only about a third of the lighting still worked. It seemed like one of those places where the owners would try and milk out as much rent as they could until they were forced with the prospect of major repairs, hoping that the forces of gentrification would drive up the price of the building, or at least allow for a premium luxury rental when the time came for either a gut rehab or just selling the building. The smell of mildew served to reinforce that suspicion. And then the smell of decay hit his nostrils.

He turned and followed his nose into the shadows where one of the overhead lights had failed. There was definitely an odor, but it didn't seem to have a source until the shadows moved. Or rather something in the shadows moved.

For a moment it was like a shift in texture. Then the thing moved forward, a mostly transparent shape that had been hidden in the gloom. As it moved closer to what passed for the light in the hall, faint details appeared on the shape. It had the appearance of an infant, perhaps four months old. It floated at chest height moving up, down and forward in a slow, unsteady motion. Its mouth was open to scream, but no sound came out.

Mister Lewis took a step back and the spectral baby continued towards him. As it left the shadows and came into what passed for the light in that gloom, the details of its appearance faded away and it was once again a transparent shape whose movement gave it away. He continued to look for the app's office and the spirit continued to follow. He was careful to walk slowly and let it keep pace.

When he found the door marked "The Wisdom of the Deceased," the security was just as tight as the front door. He turned the knob and the door opened. He reached for the light switch and just like the outer hall, only a fraction of the lights actually worked. At least the place was consistent.

There wasn't much to this office. No computers. No filing cabinets. Just a pair of heavily worn desks and a table, none of them particularly clean. It would be easy to think someone had left in a hurry, but then again, the rest of the building was in the same state of disarray as this office.

The spectral baby followed him into the office and glided into the shadows of a corner.

Upon closer examination, the table wasn't actually covered in the grime and dust of disuse. The table was covered with hair. Multiple colors of hair that Mister Lewis suspected belonged to cats. Cat hair and a few spots of blood.

That's when the hissing started.

The noise came from the shadowy corner the spectral baby had slunk into. Much as in the hall, the shadows seemed to have movement under the surface.

Mister Lewis reached into his coat pocket and produced a small mirror. Standing under one of the barely functioning lights, he angled the mirror to slightly illuminate the corner. First the spectral baby fled the corner. Next was the pale outline of a translucent cat. A second translucent cat jumped out and headed for deeper shadows across the room. The hiss repeated and a slightly more defined spectral cat floated out of the corner and landed on the table. While still mostly transparent, this cat had a slight orange hue to it. Its eyes were more defined. So were the claws it was raking over the table, with no discernable damage to the table or movement of its contents.

The orange spectral cat hissed again, baring its teeth. Then it leaned back on its hind legs, as though poised to spring.

Mister Lewis slowly stepped away and backed up towards the office's window. It was a fairly wide window as such things went and covered by blinds that were caked with what must've been at least a decade's worth of grime. He groped around for the blinds' pull cord, not taking his eyes off the cat. When he found it, he gave it a hard yank.

The windows were not particularly clean, but sunlight filled the room anyway. The spectral baby and the two colorless spectral cats disappeared with a faint popping noise.

The orange spectral cat twisted up in obvious discomfort, opened its mouth to scream and disappeared with a loud yowl.

Mister Lewis circled the room looking for more spirits but found nothing.

"Are you here for the cat?" someone had stuck their head through the partially open office door.

"What cat would that be?" Mister Lewis feigned puzzlement. "Also, who would you be?"

"Oh, I'm in the office across the hall. Are you not with the app kids?"

"No," replied Mister Lewis. "But I was looking for the Wisdom of the Deceased developers, if that's who you mean."

"I suppose you're probably too old to be with them. But yeah, they had cats in their office. They moved a couple weeks ago, and we kept hearing one of the cats."

"I can't help you with the cat," Mister Lewis shook his head. "Probably one of their experiments. You wouldn't happen to know where they moved to?"

5. In-App Upsells

The app's new office was in another building that was well past its prime, but at least it was cleaner than the last one. This time the front door was actually locked, prompting Mr. Lewis to employ the time-honored tactic of grabbing the door while someone was walking out.

The entryway was well lit, with nowhere for stray spirits to hide. He turned his head towards the office directory when the moaning started. The moaning didn't seem to be words in a particular language, just sounds of pain and anguish as it reverberated down the stairwell.

It seemed prudent to follow the groans, so up the stairwell he went. Sure enough, the groans led him to the second floor and to a door marked "Wisdom of the Deceased" by a handwritten sign taped to the door. There was nothing like the budget of a pre-seed stage startup.

The moaning was now accompanied by a banging sound, like something striking metal. The door was unlocked and opened to reveal another office with spartan décor, this time with three tech bros straight out of casting central... and a mildly decayed body strapped to a steel table that had managed to get an arm free. The body was waving that arm and periodically banging a fist on that table, all while wailing and moaning.

"Can we help you?" Tech Bro #1's voice cracked.

"We're kinda busy here," added Tech Bro #2.

"The Investor sent me," sighed Mister Lewis. "I had some questions about the source materials for your research. That thing on the table... is it part of a new app you're working on?"

"There's only one app," said Tech Bro #1. "This is an example of an in-app purchase."

"It's an upsell," added Tech Bro #3. "For an additional fee, we'd like to be able to physically raise the dead. Our estimates show a dramatic increase in Return On Investment if we implement it and we're optimistic about being able to charge 5 figures per instance."

"Are people really going to want to raise the dead if all its going to do is growl and try to eat them?" Mister Lewis furrowed his brow.

"Having the raised individual converse with the app user is going to be part of our next iteration," interjected Tech Bro #2. "Our best practices incorporate..."

"Continual improvement," Mister Lewis finished for him. "I know the drill, but isn't it a little presumptuous to be branching out into a new discipline so soon? It's troubling that you haven't even been able to establish containment in a séance and now you're trying to reanimate what are essentially zombies? Those two things are not as related as you seem to think they are."

"We don't allow negativity in this office," Tech Bro #1 screamed. "We are breaking new ground here and genius takes time to gestate."

Mister Lewis opened his mouth in rebuttal but was interrupted by the sound of a restraint ripping. He turned to see the body on the table had gotten its other arm free and was sitting up.

"Lesson one," growled Mister Lewis. "Assuming this isn't some suicide ritual I'm not familiar with, you use leather or metal restraints. The returned dead can be too strong for your basic hospital variety fabric restraints."

Tech Bro #2 grabbed at the body's flailing right wrist and missed. The body, however, didn't miss and grabbed the Bro's wrist instead. The Bro tried to twist away, but the body was stronger, which probably wasn't saying much in this instance. The body started pulling in the Bro, teeth chomping in anticipation.

As wrist neared mouth, Mister Lewis slammed a metal trash bin over the body's head. The Bro's wrist was pulled up against the side of the bin. The chomping teeth were audible from inside the bin. It was not for a lack of trying that it was unable to feed.

"Any of you guys have some salt?" said Mister Lewis as he pulled back on the trash bin and slammed the body back down on the table.

Tech Bro #3 held up a small packet, intended for French fries, doubtless from a carryout lunch.

"Nothing bigger?" asked Mister Lewis, putting all his weight on the bin as the body's arms flailed around blindly.

"This isn't a kitchen," sniffed Tech Bro #1.

"And it's a poor excuse for a morgue. How about a hammer?"

"Now that we have," said Tech Bro #3, rummaging through a desk before producing a shiny new claw hammer.

Mister Lewis released the bin and the body bolted upright again as he snatched the hammer. With his left hand, he grasped the bin and flung it off the head. Then his right hand came down hard on the body's head with the claw side of the hammer. He switched to a two-handed grip and brought the hammer down six more times until the body was still and the brains were scrambled.

"Where were we?" Mister Lewis paused for a deep breath. "You're playing around with spells that aren't as related as you think they are, and you don't have reasonable safety protocols. Did you realize you left some vestigial spirits behind at your previous office?"

"We brought our equipment with us," said Tech Bro #1. "I didn't see anything else there when we left."

"Then you weren't paying attention. These spirits were transparent, barely there and weak enough to be dispersed by exposure to daylight. Only one of them had any color to it. Your continual improvement iterations, I'm guessing. Cats and a baby."

"No, we were unable to summon those," said Tech Bro #2.

"And you didn't even know you did it," Mister Lewis facepalmed. "OK. We've established you're oblivious to anything that could have been useful. Where are you keeping the spells?"

"Spells?" asked Tech Bro #3.

"We're pioneering a new branch of science," Tech Bro #1 puffed out his chest a little.

"I don't really have time for this," Mister Lewis pulled back his arm and let fly with a backhand slap across Tech Bro #1's open mouth. "I know you were working for that slang app. I know you have a copy of the spells The Founder uploaded them. You know, the ones that got said Founder killed? The ones that might get you killed, too? I don't plan on going along for the ride. Cough them up."

"How could that get anyone killed?" asked Tech Bro #2. "Did someone get bitten?"

"Technically, yes. There are some very unpleasant, very powerful people who hoard this kind of knowledge and don't like outsiders sharing it. They raised a colony of zombie ants from the dead and those ants devoured your old boss like your little experiment tried to devour you. You're bringing that kind of attention on yourselves and I have no intention of getting sucked into the massacre that could cause. This startup is shut down."

"You'll have to buy us out," said Tech Bro #1.

"We printed out screen shots from the dictionary," said Tech Bro #2, pointing across the room. "They're over there in that desk."

Mister Lewis walked over and rifled through the desk.

"Only four pages?" he asked.

"We didn't know the app was going to get shut down," replied Tech Bro #2.

"We'd have printed all of it, otherwise," said Tech Bro #3.

"Here's part of your problem," said Mister Lewis, scanning the first page. "The Founder attempted to modernize the spells. The containment component isn't even in the summoning section. It was a cluster before you even started."

"I told you it wasn't complete," Tech Bro #3 hissed at Tech Bro #1.

"Which cloud service is this backed up to?" Mister Lewis asked the room.

"That's not secure enough for something this valuable," said Tech Bro #1 as he placed himself between Mister Lewis and a laptop on the furthest desk.

"And I'm just assuming you don't let any of the demonstration devices with the app loaded on them out of your sight?"

"Of course not," said Tech Bro #1. "And you'll have to kill me to get the code base."

"That would be easier than you think," Mister Lewis said with a smile. "It's OK. I had a feeling you were going to be that way."

Mister Lewis reached into his coat and produced a box about twice the size of a box of playing cards. It had a button on the side and a loop of wire sticking out of the end.

"Is that?" Tech Bro #1 started to ask.

"It is," Mister Lewis cut him off and pressed the button, loosing an EMP on the room.

Tech Bro #1 whirled to find the laptop unresponsive.

"Did you have to kill my phone, too?" moaned Tech Bro #3, staring in disbelief at his cell.

"Use it as an excuse to upgrade," said Mister Lewis. "I don't think you're going to be able to duplicate something you clearly didn't understand if you don't have your printouts. Forget about all of this and you might even stay alive. If you don't know the difference between raising the dead and animating a body, you have no business playing in this space. There are a lot worse things out there if you attract attention to yourselves."

Tech Bro #1 glared as Mister Lewis left the office.

In the corner of the office, two desiccated ants turned around and exited through a crack in the wall.

Delete Your Karma

1. The Bonfire of Rivals

The Salesman's nose twitched as the smell of gasoline hit it. There was getting to be a lot of it outside the house.

The house belonged to a rival. A rival with the annoying habit of posting things about him on social media. Stories about taking his clients out and getting them loaded. Stories about his clients having grand philandering adventures while their spouses thought they were at work. His clients weren't happy about it, and neither was his boss.

The stories were true, so a legal remedy was out of the question, but the stories were very inconvenient and cutting into his ability to earn a living without making certain... ethical changes that would really take the fun out of everything.

The solution had been right in front of him the whole time: kill it with fire.

The last bits of the second gas can splashed against the house. He discarded the can against the wall and fished the book of matches out of his pocket. Three matches were ripped out of the matchbook for good luck and dragged along the strike strip. He stared at the flames for a moment and then tossed them at the house.

"Note to self," muttered The Salesman as the gas lit up. "Use this on charcoal next time."

The flames wrapped around the base of the house where the gasoline had been poured and started working their way towards the sky. The Salesman approached a window and got up on his tiptoes to better peer in and see if his rival was on fire. He paused to admire his reflection in the glass and wonder if his eyes had always been this pale.

Even without the rival in view, specifically the rival's death throes in view, it was an absolutely uplifting experience. The Salesman couldn't believe he hadn't done this earlier. He inhaled deeply and exhaled slowly, then took a step back to take it all in. He was so moved by the spectacle, he failed to notice he'd perfectly framed himself for the neighbor's security camera.

After soaking it all up for a couple minutes, the sound of sirens started to drift in, and The Salesman took his leave.

2. Absolution Is Just a Click Away

"**I**f your damn app worked, he wouldn't have committed arson!"

While it wasn't all that unusual to hear screaming coming out of The Investor's office, Mister Lewis was more accustomed to hearing The Investor do the screaming and this was a different voice.

A woman he didn't recognize stormed out and didn't even bother slamming the door on the way out.

"Unsatisfied customer?" asked Mister Lewis.

"She's why you're here," replied the Investor. "Ordinarily, I'd write the whole thing off as a couple of cranks but given that there really is somebody out to get me right now, I'd like a second pair of eyes on it. You've heard of the Delete Your Karma app?"

Mister Lewis shook his head no.

"Hardly anyone has," The Investor paused for an eye roll. "It's a reputation management app. After you've entered your payment information, one click and it will clean up your reputation online."

"I thought reputation management was one part sending lawyers after the negative stories and one part writing a lot of SEO friendly new stories to push everything else to the bottom of the search engine results?" asked Mister Lewis. "You can do that with a one click app?"

"Nope," said The Investor. "Not really. I shouldn't have put money into it. I'm even the app's acting CEO right now while I decide if I'm going to shut it down or hire someone new. The app does create some posts, but they aren't very good and it doesn't really do much about the offensive posts that cause people to download it in the first place. Hardly anyone uses it anymore."

"And how does this app figure into... was it arson she was shouting about?"

"Her husband joined our illustrious list of clients. He tried the app and when it didn't achieve the desired effect, he snapped and burnt down the house of whoever had been posting about him."

"Anybody hurt?"

"Fortunately, nobody was home at the time, but the dummy was standing right in front of the neighbor's security camera," The Investor paused for a head shake. "No question who did it. Not really any question why the guy wanted everyone in the house dead, either. But the wife is claiming the guy's personality completely changed when he used the app..."

"And that sounds a little too familiar," agreed Mister Lewis. "Yeah, that's something that has to be checked out. I don't suppose that camera footage was released to the media?"

The Investor tilted the monitor around, aimed a web browser at a local TV site and they watched the view from the neighbor's security camera.

"That guy might not have a soul," remarked Mister Lewis after the footage was over.

"It really was a pretty cold thing to do," The Investor nodded.

"No," corrected Mister Lewis. "I mean that as in literal absence of a soul. And that usually means the soul has been sold."

"How the Hell can you tell that just from looking at him?" stammered the investor.

"Hell, indeed," said Mister Lewis. "I run into that more than you'd think when I consult with the music industry. After a while, you see enough of it, it just looks familiar. Some of its subtle and a little hard to articulate to a layperson, but there are a few things to look for. The subject's behavior changes and it's not too far off from psychosis. There's a lack of empathy where the soulless's goals are concerned. People become obstacles to be removed. The soulless tend to be very fixated on their goals. That really shouldn't come as a surprise. Anyone selling their soul tends to be highly motivated in the first place. And sometimes their eyes will get a little paler when the soul departs. Not always, but it's a manifestation of spiritual trauma."

"Oh. Does that mean he's coming after me?"

"Unknown. If he sold his soul, my guess is he did it for revenge. That might not have anything to do with you or it might've been more of a blanket vengeance against everyone who ever wronged him. If its blanket revenge and his wife isn't the only one who's mad your app didn't work... then it's possible you got added to his list. If not, you might not have anything to worry about as long as you're not in between him and the targets of vengeance. Even if you did fall under a blanket revenge, it seems unlikely this would be the work of whoever's been targeting you. Selling souls is infernal magic. That's a different world than what we've been seeing."

"And if I or my company gets crossed up with whoever he wants revenge on?" The Investor was developing a slight twitch.

"Things standing in the direct path between the soulless and their vengeance tend to get squashed. Infernal revenge magic can be a runaway train. Unless you have a way to countervail it, it's best to stay out of the way."

"This is something you can stop?"

"I have before. Assuming that's what this is. I need to check it out. If the deal wasn't negotiated properly, he could... burn himself out... before I can lay hands on him. Or the acts of vengeance could go on for a while and I might be obligated to step in. Someone sells their soul for fame, it's generally cleaner to let things run their course. The soulless will get their real reward in the end, after the contract has ended. Revenge is messy, though. Sometimes you can't mind your own business with that."

"Does that mean I don't have to pay the full fee if this is a revenge case against someone else?" a hint of a smile passed The Investor's lips.

"Only if you want to forgo me checking it out in the first place. Of course, if you did end up in his path, either by intent or accident, that means I wouldn't be here to run interference. Probably harder to do crisis management PR without insights into what happened, too."

"Go," The Investor shrugged. "I'm not sure this app has life in it, but I suppose there's always the fund to think about. Nothing's stuck to us in the press so far, but too many more of these unexplained events around our periphery and it could affect future confidence."

"That does seem like it could be part of someone's plan," Mister Lewis said on his way out the door.

3. Down in Flames

If The Salesman had sold his soul for revenge, Mister Lewis reasoned that he'd still be obsessed with killing his rival, so the best way to look for The Salesman would be to look for his rival. Since it was early afternoon, he set off for the rival's office, located on the third floor of a dilapidated four-story office building.

Giving the outside of the building the once over, he crossed into the alley next to it and followed the alley to the rear. That was where he saw someone climbing the fire escape. It wasn't hard to follow, but the man had a three-story lead.

When he got to the roof, sure enough, there was The Salesman, trying to take the cap off a can of gasoline.

"Cooking at high altitudes causes food to lose moisture faster," said Mister Lewis as he came off the ladder. "It can crisp too fast and then the inside doesn't cook evenly."

"Are you nuts?" snarled The Salesman. "We're only forty feet off the ground. Fifty, tops. This isn't high altitude. And I'm not cooking."

"How could you not be thinking about grilling on a day like this?" Mister Lewis gestured widely while staring into The Salesman's pale eyes.

"There might be some meat cooking. Wait... who the Hell are you?"

"Just someone who needs to check on a couple things before you're about your business," Mister Lewis took two steps closer.

"Check somewhere else," The Salesman managed to get the cap off the gas can. He threw that cap at Mister Lewis and stepped backwards towards the middle of the roof.

"It's alright," Mister Lewis continued to advance. "I'm familiar with the standard contract. I just want to know what you sold for."

"Sold what?" The Salesman retreated further.

"Your soul. It's really obvious you're no longer in possession of your soul. What were the terms? Wealth? Fame? Revenge?"

"The Hell are you talking about?" The Salesman stopped and frowned.

"Yes, that's what I'm talking about. You're up here for revenge?"

"Well... fine. If you want to call it that, fine. Now keep back."

"Oh, trust me," Mister Lewis stopped and raised his hands. "I'm familiar with revenge contracts. I would prefer not to get between you and your contractually designated target. Is it a single target? If it's a single target, you're casting kind of a wide net setting the entire building on fire. Tell me about the contract."

"I like fire," The Salesman fumbled for his book of matches. "Why don't you take your crazy talk and get out of here? You're freaking me out."

"So, fire was part of the contract," Mister Lewis stepped forward again. "You know there are sometimes ways to void a contract? It's not easy, but I have some…"

"Stop talking," screamed The Salesman. "I don't need more distractions."

Holding the gas can in the crook of his left arm, The Salesman held the matchbook in his left hand as he struck the three matches with his right hand. As the matches ignited, he lost his grip on the gas can, which tumbled forward splashing his shirt and pants, and leaving him standing in a small, but growing puddle as it landed on its side.

"Dammit," yelled The Salesman as he instinctively patted at the wet shirt with his left hand. "Look what you made me do."

And then he fumbled the matches.

The first match lit his shirt. And a half second later, the last two matches hit the puddle of gasoline at his feet. The Salesman was lit.

The scream wasn't particularly coherent as the Salesman panicked and tried to run. Unfortunately, blindly running on a roof is seldom advisable and his path took him tumbling over the side of the roof.

By the time Mister Lewis got to the side of the roof to peer down, the flaming body was already starting to draw a crowd. It wasn't moving and Mister Lewis figured that scorched blood was going to be very annoying to scrub clean.

"That couldn't have been in the contract," he muttered to himself as he fled the roof before someone could think to check where the flaming body had come from.

4. Kill Switch

"I can guarantee that man had no soul," said Mister Lewis.

"So, it's over," asked The Investor. "He sold his soul to get revenge and you killed him. That has to end it, right?"

"That's not how it works," Mister Lewis. "I didn't really kill him, either. He got spooked and dropped his matches. Honestly, that's strange enough on its own, but that's not what's bothering me. If you sign a contract for revenge, you get your revenge unless the contract is undone. If you set yourself on fire and fall off a building, you'd normally get back up and go on with your plan. Now... if you already happened to be on fire when you enacted your revenge, you might well burn to death immediately afterwards. There's a sort of gallows humor with the contract administrators and they'd certainly think that was funny. Setting yourself on fire, falling off a building and just going splat? That would be breach of contract. It just doesn't happen."

"Are you sure he's still dead?" asked The Investor. "Is this one of those things where he wakes up in the morgue and goes back to work?"

"No, I checked up on that before heading back. He's dead. Not really enough of his head left to reanimate, either, since zombies keep popping up. That leaves us with a man relieved of his soul plotting murder and arson while in the orbit of one of your apps. Unlikely to be a coincidence."

Shouting from the outer office put the conversation on pause. In short order, the door burst open, and The Salesman's wife burst in again.

"You did this," she screamed at The Investor. "Now he's dead. He was fine until he used your stupid app. What do you have to say for yourself now?"

The Investor reddened but kept silent.

"What exactly do you think happened?" asked Mister Lewis.

"I'll show you what happened," screamed The Salesman's wife. "I still have his phone."

She held up a phablet phone as though it were a trophy, then brought it down and started swiping the screen.

"First he opened that app," she continued with no decibel spared. "See? Here it is. Here's his name. See? It's all filled out. Then he pressed this button to make all those libelous posts go away. See?"

The Salesman's wife pressed the button with a little too much theatrical flair. She paused, glared at the phone and made a show of pressing it again.

"This damn thing doesn't want to connect," she muttered while pressing it a third time. "Oh, now it's working."

Then she screamed. Her body went rigid as though electrical current was running through it. Her eyes opened wide and the color in her iris faded.

"You destroyed him," The Salesman's wife snarled at The Investor. "I'll destroy you. I'll destroy your company. It can all burn to the ground just like he burned."

"I think you can leave now," Mister Lewis stepped in front of The Investor.

The Salesman's wife threw the phone at Mister Lewis, who was only too happy to catch it.

"Thank you," said Mister Lewis. "I was wanting a look at that. You can still leave. Now."

The two stared at each other for a bit before The Salesman's wife let out one last scream and stormed out.

"What just happened?" asked The Investor.

"We just found out what happened to your client's soul," said Mister Lewis, holding the phone up to the light. "This is worse than I thought."

"What are you talking about?"

"You know how this app's named Delete Your Karma?"

"Yes?"

"This app has also been cursed. Instead of deleting karma, it appears to have deleted her soul."

"How is that even possible?" moaned The Investor.

"It's not easy," replied Mister Lewis. "The trigger must be similar to that reality show gaming app curse. It was activated by a button in the app."

"A mouseover of doom," groaned The Investor.

"Close enough. It didn't kick off until she tried to submit the order, specifically when the app connected to the server. You need to shut that server down, immediately. Take the trigger offline."

"I'll shutter the entire startup behind the app," The Investor said while staring blankly into space. "The damn thing never worked in the first place. There are barely any users. I'll take a write-off on it. Rip off the bandage. At least a tax benefit will be something positive to come out of this."

"How many users has this thing had in the last month?"

"Two," The Investor hit a few keys and turned to the printer. "This is all the contact information on the other person still using it. Looks like the account is two weeks old."

"I'll go and see if he's been compromised. While I do that, you need to call the police."

"Why would I ever want to involve the police in any of this?" asked The Investor.

"You call the police and tell them that woman threatened to kill you. What you need to understand is that she wasn't joking. Her soul's been destroyed. She can't get better from that. Once the soulless get fixated on you, that fixation sticks until they've done what they set out to do. It got her husband killed. She's not going to pass a psych evaluation if they mention your name. They'll have her committed. Otherwise, she will come after you."

"If she's trying to kill me, is there a more direct approach?" asked The Investor.

"That woman is a victim," Mister Lewis's voice was close to a whisper. "She hasn't been killed and reanimated, she's still alive. Damaged, but alive. Without a soul, when she dies, she just ends. Magic doesn't get blacker than what's happened here. I will find who's doing this and I will stop it, but I'm not going to assassinate her for you. You need to have her locked up and committed."

Mister Lewis took the paper with the final user's address and walked out.

The Investor remained seated, lost in nervous contemplation.

5. Puppets Without Strings

The front door of The Mechanic's house swung open in slow motion. Reaching the end of its arc, it stayed in place for a few moments and then Mister Lewis walked in.

The front door led to the living room and it was empty. Empty and silent as a tomb. Mister Lewis pressed forward through the living room into the kitchen. It, too, was empty. Could it be that no one was home?

He moved back to the living room, his eyes surveying the stairs to the second floor when a voice rang out.

"Stand at attention when I talk to you!"

There was an edge in the voice, but it didn't seem like a threat, so Mister Lewis decided to see where things were going and straightened up a bit. He turned his head to face the stairs and caught a glimpse of feet just visible near the top of the flight. The feet weren't moving, so he turned and took a step towards the stairs.

"Stop where you are," barked the voice.

He paused after a step and waited. The feet moved down the staircase, revealing a man with ageless features who could have been 40 or 70, wearing a Nehru jacket and holding a mobile phone with a small wooden statue tied to it.

"I have a mission for you," said the man on the stairs as he fondled the statue. "Someone for you to destroy."

"That sort of thing is expensive," replied Mister Lewis. "Let's hear your offer."

The man on the stairs glared and inhaled deeply enough to make a show of it.

"My offer is to accept your worship," which was followed by a theatrical exhale that was meant to convey superiority.

"There are rates for these things," Mister Lewis took a step forward. "Give me the details and I'll give you an estimate."

"Stand still," bellowed the man on the stairs, holding the phone out in front of him. "You will destroy a swine who revels in money and wrecking lives."

"That doesn't exactly narrow it down," Mister Lewis saw the Delete Your Karma app displayed on the phone's screen and his eyes narrowed.

"You will not ask questions," the man's bellowing raised half an octave. "A money lender must be humiliated and then put down."

Mister Lewis took another step towards the stairs.

"Stop," screamed the man on the stairs.

Mister Lewis stopped. He wondered how fast the man was and how much closer he could get before the man would start running?

"Why won't the damn server connect?" muttered the man as he swiped madly at his phone's screen.

"The server's probably down," replied Mister Lewis.

"It should not be this difficult to avenge a child," the man said to himself, lost in thought and anxiety.

"Yeah," said Mister Lewis. "It really would be a lot easier if you weren't busy trying to manufacture living zombies in order to stay under The Necromancers' radar. That's got to slow things down."

"Who are you?" whispered the man on the stairs, his eyes narrowing.

"And it doesn't seem like it's working very well," Mister Lewis continued. "You did end up killing those kids with the gaming app, so you're not under their radar anymore."

"You're with the council," the man backed up a step.

"No," Mister Lewis shook his head. "But we've had two conversations, so far. The last one was on the dock as your little army was trying to figure out how to swim. The first one was when some reanimated ants had a feast."

"Assassin!" The man's eyes lit up.

"No," replied Mister Lewis, raising his open palms in a gesture of innocence. "I was trying to talk the kid down. I wasn't fast enough. Personally, I didn't think it warranted how it went down, but you know that crowd. They have very strict rules, and it was incredibly stupid putting those books online."

"Who do you work for?" hissed the man on the stairs.

"The Investor behind that startup."

"That's who set this in motion," growled the man. "Pressure to make unrealistic audience numbers. Pressure to pivot. Succeed or be fired. Never mind who created the company. Never mind whose dreams are stolen. Without those threats, my books are never stolen and none of this happens."

"Those necromancers were wondering where those books came from," said Mister Lewis. "They're not real happy with you. I'm not either. Look, I'm sorry about the kid, but there's no act of discipline where destroying souls is remotely acceptable. You've crossed everyone's line with this stunt. It stops now."

"It stops when your Investor is ruined and dead. In that order. Humiliation, then death. My child was humiliated and emotionally tortured before death. There will be symmetry."

"Look," Mister Lewis sighed. "The vampires were a nice touch. I'll give you that. If that went on a couple more days, you could have taken a bite out of the bottom line and made that app into a public pariah... all while keeping things at arm's length. This current scam... you realize that's probably the least popular app in The Investor's portfolio? It's had two users in the last month and I watched the first one fall to his death yesterday. You don't have an army. You can't damage finances that don't exist. It's not working."

"Then I suppose I can do it the easy way if they're aware of me and there's no longer any point to remaining in the shadows."

"Or you could just shut up and come with me," Mister Lewis crossed over to the foot of the stairs. "The Necromancers would like to talk to you, and they don't really care what condition I deliver you in."

The sound of a door slamming shut came from the front of the house, followed by footsteps. The Mechanic was home.

"Who the Hell are you two and why are you in my house?" screamed The Mechanic.

"I command you," the man on the stairs once more raised the phone and statue. "Kill this man."

The Mechanic froze.

The man on the stairs smiled.

"How about I kick both your asses?" said The Mechanic.

"Does nothing work the way it's supposed to?" howled the man on the stairs as he hurled his phone at The Mechanic.

The Mechanic grunted and charged the stairs.

The man on the stairs stepped backwards towards the top of the stairs.

Mister Lewis hit the first step in pursuit and realized he was about to be tackled by The Mechanic. Turning, he managed to catch The Mechanic in a front headlock, but The Mechanic's momentum carried him into the wall.

He brought a knee up, catching The Mechanic in the head, but it didn't have much effect. The Mechanic sneered, grabbed the lapels of Mister Lewis's jacket and threw him.

Mister Lewis was trying to decide if The Mechanic was just that strong or it was the strength that comes from adrenaline and a total lack of self-control as he rolled back to his feet.

The Mechanic charged again. The nearest handy object was a small coffee table, so Mister Lewis grabbed that and smacked him in the face with it. The coffee table tore apart, revealing itself to be mostly particle board. Its effect was more irritation than bodily harm.

The Mechanic swung a wild right hook. Mister Lewis blocked and followed through with a kick to the groin.

That, the Mechanic felt as the air went out of him, and he doubled over.

Mister Lewis glanced around, and his eyes settled on a brass lamp of medium weight. He grabbed it and swung the lamp's base down on The Mechanic's head. The Mechanic hit the floor, not quite unconscious, but not likely to cause a problem for a few minutes.

Mister Lewis ran up the stairs, but his quarry had left during the fight. A window was open and the carpet at the end of the hall had a scorch mark shaped roughly like a circle. It was hard to say which was the entrance and which was the exit.

6. The Digital Cleanse

M ister Lewis entered The Investor's office and said nothing. The Investor, fearing bad news, also said nothing.

"Bad news," Mister Lewis finally broke the silence. "I think I know who's got it in for you."

"Who?"

"You got a picture of that dead Founder's Father handy?"

The Investor pecked away at the computer and then turned the monitor.

"Yeah, that's your problem," said Mister Lewis with a sigh. "I was pretty sure that's who he was, but I needed to make sure he didn't send a proxy."

"You met him?"

"Not long ago. Sure enough, he was trying to... prog ram... your last privacy app user into taking you out. I'd have ended it right there and then, but the last user came home and tried to jump me. The Founder's Father took off while we scuffled."

"What did you do with my customer?"

"Nothing you need to know about," replied Mister Lewis. "Poor bastard isn't likely to be bothering you. You're not his beef."

"What did The Father want?"

"Revenge," replied Mister Lewis. "He's as much mad at himself as he is at you, but you're getting his share of the blame, too. He thinks you humiliated his kid into putting those spell books online in a desperate attempt to not get fired."

"That's ridiculous," said The Investor.

"It wasn't too far off what the kid told me before The Necromancers showed up," continued Mister Lewis. "But there's not much we can do about that now. Turns out those books belonged to The Founder's Father, so he's probably projecting his guilt onto you for being the gateway to what got his kid killed. He wants you dead, but he wants you broken and humiliated first, just like he thinks his kid was."

"You can't let him do that!"

"It's my job to keep you alive," said Mister Lewis. "But in order to do that, you're going to have to take a short-term financial hit."

"What do you mean by that?" said the Investor, cheeks reddening.

"The last thing he said to me was he didn't have to hide in the shadows anymore. What's he been doing? Bending over backwards, trying to curse your apps in such a way that The Necromancers wouldn't see him operating. It didn't work very well, but it still caused plenty of trouble. It's also pretty technically complex magic. I don't doubt he'd be a lot more efficient using more... conventional means."

"You make your point, but what is the actionable plan?"

"Shut down your investment portfolio. All the apps. The whole thing needs to go offline."

"Interrupt continuity of service?"

"He's likely to curse everything left in your portfolio," said Mister Lewis. "He's going to want to make a public display of it. Ruin your finances, wreck your companies and then once you have nothing left, come for you. Quite possibly with your own reanimated customers."

"Shutting down the portfolio really could ruin my finances, too," whispered The Investor. "Undermine confidence in my apps. Cut off my cash flow."

"I don't think this guy will interpret that as a humiliation at his hands," replied Mister Lewis. "He clearly wants to twist the knife. Shut it down on your own terms so you can spin things back up after I've dealt with him or The Necromancers catch up with him. Remember, I'm not the only one looking for him and he's not going to be able to hide from The Necromancers very long if he starts operating overtly."

"It's not like I have a kill switch for my businesses," The Investor stalled. "This is going to take some time."

"Then you better hope it's going to take The Founder's Father some time, too, otherwise we could be drowning in a sea of the recently deceased."

Massively Multiplayer
Online Resurrection Game

1. Extra Life

The goblins were swarming. The Player swung a mighty broadsword. Two goblins fell, but four more surged forward.

Outside the game, The Player swiped madly at the screen of the smartphone. This was the furthest The Player had ever gotten in the game and a new high score was looming.

Inside the game, The Player was spinning in a circle with the broadsword cutting down anything that came into its path. Five more goblins dropped, but twenty more massed in a circle just beyond the blade's arc.

Outside the game, a bead of sweat worked its way down The Player's brow, into the corner of the eye. The Player blinked in discomfort, right hand leaving the phone to wipe at the eye.

Inside the game, The Player stopped spinning. The Goblins descended.

Outside the game, The Player was swiping blindly with the left thumb while trying to clear the eye. After a few seconds, the right hand returned to the phone.

Inside the game, The Player was starting to spin, but it was too late. The last goblin reached its target, and the life force bar ran dry. The score was just shy of an extra life as The Player fell.

Outside the game, The Player frowned and then inhaled deeply in preparation for an exercise in creative swearing. Mid-inhalation, The Player's eyes went wide. Air rattled in the throat. The phone fell to the ground and The Player followed it, collapsing in a lifeless pile.

Inside the game, The Player had just missed an extra life. Outside the game, The Player was both more and less fortunate. The Player rose again, but there was no life in the eyes. The Player shambled towards the door to play a role in a different kind of bonus level.

2. Staged Retreat

"How many are left?" asked Mister Lewis.

"I just finished removing Goblin Gusher from the sales platform," The Investor was bent over the keyboard. "They only let you take these down one at a time if you want to still get paid, and I will be paid."

"How many are left?" asked Mister Lewis.

"Three," replied The Investor. "Music in the Cloud, Collect the Monsters and Mindful SelfCare. And then I still have to pull them from the servers. That will go a little faster. At least I've got my own servers for some of them."

"It all has to come down," said Mister Lewis. "It still isn't clear if he's cursing new downloads or the use of the existing apps. It can all go back online after we've dealt with him."

"It's not going to be fun explaining this if anyone asks what happened to revenue and user growth," growled The Investor.

"There's another way to approach it," said Mister Lewis. "Ask yourself: what's the lifetime value of a dead customer?"

3. The Sound and the Slurry

The Listener tapped at the smartphone's screen. The music wasn't coming from the cloud anymore. What use was something called "Music in the Cloud" if nothing was coming out of the cloud? Music was no longer falling from the sky like a warm spring drizzle, and all was not right with the world.

A noise flickered in the left earbud. A slight sputtering sound that quickly vanished.

The Listener responded by cranking the phone's volume up to 100%.

Nothing was there.

The Listener reverted to the app's playlist. Three songs were tapped on, three songs failed to connect. The phone was definitely online. Email worked. The web browser worked. And then the screen changed.

The Music In the Cloud app announced it was playing something called "Just Rewards."

An instant later, an immersive sound came through the earbuds. And something else came, too. The Listener could feel something hot crawling through the ear. Pain flashed as the tympanic membrane was pierced, but the crawling thing kept moving inward.

Then it hit the auditory nerve, The Listener collapsed to the floor, writhed for a bit and then lay still.

Five minutes later, The Listener rose again, this time, head tilted to let a slurry of blood, brain fluid and organic matter drip out. Once the head was drained, The Listener staggered towards the door.

4. Heal Thyself

The Disciple of Fads was feeling down. But that was OK. The Mindful SelfCare app was the new new thing, much better than the old new thing, and was sure to erase the blues. The app was downloaded and ready to launch.

The app displayed "How are you feeling?" and offered three colors for the response.

The Disciple tapped on the blue square.

"Run with scissors!" appeared on the screen in reply to the input.

The Disciple pondered for a moment, thought "why not," and began digging around through drawers for scissors. When the scissors were found, three laps around the apartment followed.

The app had reverted to the "How are you feeling?" screen. The Disciple contemplated this question and tapped the blue square again.

"Do you have vodka?" displayed on the screen.

Now this was the sort of mindfulness The Disciple of Fads could really get behind. The app had very detailed instructions for a series of shots that escalated in both size and speed. The Disciple was only too happy to comply.

Post-vodka, The Disciple glanced down at the app. "How are you feeling?" had returned to the screen. Alas, the Disciple was not a happy drunk and the mood darkened as it took four attempts to successfully tap on the blue square.

"Run with scissors!" returned to the screen.

The scissors were already out, which made it an easy enough suggestion to follow.

On the second lap around the apartment, The Disciple of Fads stumbled and fell, embedding the scissors in the throat. At least the vodka served to dull the pain.

The Disciple rolled around a bit. Between the booze and the slickness of the blood, it was too hard to get up.

The Disciple of Fad's eyes closed for what should have been the last time. They only stayed closed for five minutes. When the eyes opened again, there was a distinct lack of vitality to them. While the ability to stand up didn't seem impaired by alcohol, the stagger towards the door was indistinguishable from a lush's gait.

5. Theory and Philosophy of Apps

"**J**ust one more and we're done," The Investor looked up from the keyboard.

"Glad to hear it," replied Mister Lewis. "By the way, since the curse is manifesting as a perverse extension of these apps, I've been looking at your catalog as you take them offline. Aren't most of them fairly derivative of more famous apps?"

"That's the point," said The Investor. "Why waste money on market research when you can let somebody else do it for you? If an app is successful, they've identified an opportunity and they've probably screwed up at least three things groping around in the dark for a market. You study the original app, study the market and then become a disrupter. In the best-case scenario, you improve the experience and poach the first app's user base."

"And there's good money in that?"

"Not always," said The Investor. "Sometimes you can't chip away at the original. But often enough you can reach part of the market the original didn't or find a new segment. It's always more efficient knowing who you're going after. Sometimes you can ramp up fast and sell the app. Sometimes you become the market standard. Originality is a much more risky investment than cloning. Everybody loves a bandwagon."

"As long as you're off the wagon before it crashes," replied Mister Lewis.

"Exactly," agreed The Investor. "Pull your money out early and then go bargain hunting amidst the rubble after the market collapses. There's always something interesting that gets caught short in a crash."

"The jackal as a business model. I suppose there will always be a place for scavengers in the world."

"Most people in my profession prefer to think of it as identifying opportunities and inefficiencies," The Investor frowned. "At least you aren't using that awful Vulture Capital meme. That's a very hurtful meme. There, the last app is off the server. What do we do now?"

"We wait," said Mister Lewis. "If we're lucky, we cut those off before he could let loose with whatever he was planning. In that case, I can go back to hunting him. That should be a little easier now that I know who I'm looking for."

"And if we weren't fast enough?"

"If the curse falls on apps that are already installed on devices and running without a server connection, something will likely come knocking on your door before I have a chance to hunt."

6. A Hunting We Will Go

The Mighty Hunter peered through the smartphone and there were monsters all around. It had been a productive morning and three monsters had been collected: AnnaPhlaxis, Occipipus and Lardomic. That was not good enough. Somewhere in the park was Goobermatix, an ancient and powerful monster that would complete the collection.

The Mighty Hunter glanced up from the phone. The route to Goobermatix led up a steep tree-lined hill. There was a path to follow... barely, so up the hill The Mighty Hunter trudged. Presumably, at the top of the hill would be the monster pit. When The Mighty Hunter stepped into the same space as the pit in the real world, the app on the smartphone would match the geographic coordinates and open the pit in the game, allowing a great battle to ensue.

Not quite to the top, The Mighty Hunter paused. The phone was held up and the Collect the Monsters app swiped at to check the inventory of monster traps. It was also a good excuse to catch one's breath. This was a bit more of a hike than The Mighty Hunter was used to.

And then Goobermatix moved. Or rather the location of the monster pit containing Goobermatix moved. This was not something that normally happened.

Suspecting a glitch, The Mighty Hunter closed and reopened the map. Sure enough, Goobermatix had moved. Indeed, the app seemed to indicate Goobermatix was walking away. The Mighty Hunter had been looking to complete the collection and could not tolerate the thought of the last prize creature escaping.

And this was how The Mighty Hunter came to be sprinting up the hill, alternating between glancing at the screen to follow Goobermatix's retreat and looking up to dodge trees. It was unfortunate that the last tree that needed dodging was concealing a lovely view of a cliff and the rocks below.

The Mighty Hunter's next footfall found air where there should have been hill. After a drop of twenty feet and a collision with rocky ground, the tumbling began, bouncing off trees and logs before coming to rest at the bottom.

Amazingly, the smartphone was still in one piece. The app recorded the location as coinciding with the monster pit and Goobermatix appeared on the screen.

No monster traps were flung at Goobermatix.

The Mighty Hunter's head was facing the wrong direction to see the screen, even if the rest of the body was oriented towards it.

Goobermatix escaped inside the world of the app.

Back in the real world, The Mighty Hunter stirred. Reanimation was a harsh process but having your head facing the wrong direction made for an even harsher adjustment. Eventually, The Mighty Hunter came around to embrace the difficult task of staggering backwards so that whatever light that could still pass through those lifeless eyes would guide the way.

7. The Player Magnet

"How long do we wait?" asked The Investor.

"Let's give it another hour," replied Mister Lewis. "If he was serious about reverting to the original plan, trouble can't be far off. If I'm wrong and it's all clear in an hour, we'll get you locked down and I'll go looking for him. I'm not going to leave you alone unless I know the first wave isn't imminent."

"How do I lock down when we don't know what's coming?" The Investor fidgeted behind the desk.

"I'm working on that," replied Mister Lewis. "I'm inclined to think it's going to be another form of undead attack. Most of the variations on reanimated bodies that might get thrown at you won't be able to swim, so we might put you on a boat. Vampires don't like water, either, but I don't think he'll be able to play that card a second time. But if he could actually get control of a still living and thinking human, they can pilot a boat."

"Wouldn't they have to find me first?" asked The Investor.

"If he could have reanimated bodies converging on The Reality Star, he can have them converging on you. He's not hiding anymore, so we have to assume whatever comes next will be an established spell that he's done before and works as intended."

"I should probably give the other investors in my venture fund a heads up about the app outage," The Investor produced a smartphone.

"Not until this is over," Mister Lewis snatched the phone. "You should keep your distance from anything with an app on it. I suspect he wants you to see your death coming, but you might have a curse waiting for you on that phone."

"And thus, my business is further disrupted," The Investor's brow furrowed. "This feels like letting the terrorists win."

Mister Lewis's reply was preempted by a scream from the outer office.

Rushing to the door, they found staff scattering as a disheveled figure lumbered through the desks. It was walking backwards because its head was on backwards and it needed to see where it was going.

"Back to the reanimated corpses," muttered Mister Lewis. "Stay here."

Mister Lewis calmly walked up to the corpse, which seemed to notice him.

In response to his presence, the corpse tried to grasp him. Alas, the corpse could not reach Mister Lewis. Because it was walking backwards, its arms were attempting to reach backwards, and they just didn't bend back far enough to be effective.

The corpse turned to give its arms a chance to grasp Mister Lewis, but its head couldn't pivot with the body – it stayed staring straight ahead, so the arms flayed around blindly. Mister Lewis merely stepped sideways.

The corpse backed up a few more steps, walking in a straight line towards the Investor's office.

Mister Lewis circled behind the corpse. The corpse seemed to notice him but had a terrible reaction time. Before it could turn, he'd grabbed its head and started twisting. Once he'd gotten it turned around to its natural position facing front, he applied a headlock and twisted through until it was facing backwards again. One more turn and the head came loose.

"You're going to need to get that dry cleaned," The Investor pointed to where the corpse's removed head was dripping blood and fluids onto Mister Lewis's suit coat.

"That's why I always wear black," replied Mister Lewis as he kicked the corpse's body to the ground. "Easier to clean and it doesn't show quite as much when I'm leaving an incident. You don't want to wear a lot of white in this business. It really is convenient when they show up with a broken neck, though. So much easier to finish the job that way."

The body on the floor stopped flailing. Mister Lewis released the head, dropping it into a trash can, then walked over the window.

"That's what I was afraid of," he said while peering through the glass. "Whatever our rogue necromancer is doing, it's not happening in a vacuum. Have a look."

The Investor did as asked and saw another staggering person in the building's parking lot and two more coming off the street. A week before, they might have been written off as drunks or junkies, but The Investor was starting to become familiar with the freshly dead.

"How many will come?" asked The Investor.

"Hard to say," replied Mister Lewis. "We never did figure out what kind of a physical radius his spells encompass. It seems likely he's still targeting the users of your apps, whether it's fresh downloads or not. The equation we're looking at is probably looking at spell radius times user density."

"That could be a lot," whispered The Investor.

"If we're lucky, shutting down those apps cut off his supply of new troops... or at least slowed down their creation."

"How long do we have to last to find that out?" asked The Investor.

"As long as it takes," replied Mister Lewis. "I think it's time to move you, though. Let's go to your car. The dead aren't great with moving targets."

They met another walking corpse in the hallway. Mister Lewis shattered its kneecap with a kick. It kept following but dragging one leg on top of a semi-coordinated stagger meant it was moving much more slowly than Mister Lewis and The Investor were walking. They left it behind as they took the stairs down to the first floor.

The parking lot was not particularly full of the ambulatory deceased. Perhaps 15 of them were wandering in the general direction of the building.

"What did you drive today?" asked Mister Lewis.

The Investor pointed toward a Hummer parked in the front row towards the back of the building.

"Congratulations," said Mister Lewis. "It's not every day somebody has a practical use for a Hummer in a city environment."

They walked quickly to the Hummer and piled in. As they did, the corpses altered their paths to head towards the vehicle.

"Are they going to pen us in?" The Investor checked the rearview mirror with alarm.

"Doesn't matter," replied Mister Lewis. "Not in this. If you can't avoid them, go through a couple of them. It's not like you're going to kill them. They're not stacked up anywhere deep enough yet to actually stop you if you drop the pedal."

"Yet?"

"It would be better if we got out of the parking lot before it fills up."

The Investor backed out of the parking spot a bit too quickly, but nothing quite tipped over.

The corpses were getting closer, but they weren't converging in an even, organized pattern. The Investor veered right, moved over a row in the parking lot and then gunned the Hummer in a beeline for the exit. While they were able to avoid the bulk of the forming crowd, one body did bounce off the front bumper before they cleared the lot.

"Where do I go now?" The Investor came to a stop on the street just outside the parking lot.

"Go left for a couple blocks," Mister Lewis was looking out the passenger side window and noticing a dense mob of at least 20 of the recently deceased heading in their direction.

The Investor pumped the gas and slammed on the breaks after two blocks, then turned and struck an intensely quizzical pose.

"I don't like this," muttered Mister Lewis. "There seemed to be an awful lot of them showing up quickly. We might not have shut things down fast enough."

"Or all the installed apps are cursed," The Investor's eyes widened.

"That's a possibility. I probably need to talk to those Necromancers sooner than later. This is looking like their size of a problem."

"Where are they?" The Investor's hands tightened on the steering wheel.

"Everywhere and nowhere," sighed Mister Lewis. "OK. New plan. Let's go another half mile in this direction, then take a left and go 10 blocks or so... until you find a good place to park. One we can get out of in a hurry. We'll wait 10 minutes or until the corpses start showing up. Let's see if we can draw them in the wrong direction and buy a little more time. The instant we see one, head another couple blocks west and double back to The Founder's house."

"The Founder?" stammered The Investor. "Is the Founder one of these zombies chasing us?"

"The Founder's home is a place the Necromancers are definitely watching. I'm hoping I can get their attention if we show up. They knew how to shut down the last mass outbreak quickly. Otherwise... I guess we'll start by getting you on a boat."

The tires squealed as The Investor dropped the pedal again.

8. Where the Dead Things Live

The gate to The Founder's back yard inched open and Mister Lewis slid in. A quick survey suggested it was unchanged from his last visit and he motioned The Investor to follow.

"That's where The Necromancers sent me to find the fetish that was controlling the undead mob sent after The Reality Star," Mister Lewis gestured to the middle of the yard. "And that's where I destroyed it. Let's just stand where we know they've been looking, and they should eventually check in."

They moved toward the center of the yard. Mister Lewis lifted his head skyward and waved his arms in the air.

"Is this where The Founder died?" asked The Investor.

"Within a couple feet," replied Mister Lewis, not lowering his head.

"Because that kinda looks like the Founder," The Investor pointed towards the open back door of the house.

Inside the house, a figure, back to the doorway, stood over someone seated in a chair, doing something to the seated person's head.

"It does," Mister Lewis whispered, lowering his gaze from the sky.

The pair of them slowly moved toward the door.

Sure enough, it was The Founder in the chair. Or at least what was left of The Founder's body, heavily bandaged. The figure leaning over it was stuffing something through an open flap of heavily decayed skin at the top of The Founder's skull.

"I've got this," The Investor held a banded stack of twenty-dollar bills.

"Don't" began Mister Lewis, but he was too late.

The Investor threw the money at the figure, striking him in the back. The bills bounced off and fell to the ground.

"That only works on vampires," sighed Mister Lewis.

The figure turned to face them, revealing him to be The Founder's Father, who glared at The Investor and then glanced down at the money.

"Did you try to kill me with money?" The Founder's Father was struggling to retain composure. "Do you not have any other response mechanism? With your resources? I suppose that's why I was planning on it being the death of you. Oh, well... you're here, so you can die a little sooner."

The Founder's Father raised his hands above his head and gestured. Up from the ground behind Mister Lewis and The Investor sprang a half-decayed body.

"You didn't think I wasn't prepared for guests?" leered The Founder's Father.

The corpse was particularly spritely for something less than whole. It lunged at The Investor, but Mister Lewis caught it by the throat and threw it back.

"I'm prepared for many guests," The Founder's Father gestured again, and another body shot up through the ground. This one was a little fresher.

Mister Lewis kicked the new body in the chest, knocking it back into the first corpse and tangling them in a pile. His eyes darted around the yard and settled on a spade that was leaning against the fence behind The Investor.

"Toss me that," he said, gesturing toward the spade.

"Third time lucky," The Founder's Father repeated the gesture and a third body emerged from the ground. This one was wet from putrification.

The Investor tossed the spade. Mister Lewis caught it and pivoted to swing the spade at the oozing corpse's neck. The spade passed through, the head came off and the body fell to the ground.

"The wandering mob of your former customers will be here soon," The Founder's Father called to The Investor.

Mister Lewis lifted the spade over his head and brought it down in an arch on the skull of the first corpse. The skull split and the corpse collapsed.

"Last time he had a fetish bound to a phone controlling the dead," Mister Lewis yelled at The Investor.

The Founder's Father merely laughed.

The fresh corpse lumbered toward Mister Lewis, who took its legs out from under it with the spade before bringing its blade down on the corpse's neck three times. Eventually, the head rolled free.

"I don't see any phones," screamed The Investor.

"We can keep this up all night," The Founder's Father gestured yet again, and a fourth corpse appeared, then a fifth. "I'm not hiding anymore. There's no fetish for you to burn. As far as the likes of you are concerned, I am a living fetish. I control my army without the aid of trinkets."

A thin smile broke out on Mister Lewis's face as he dropped the spade and sank his fingers into the hair of the fresh corpse's detached head. He shifted his hip and hurled the head sidearm. It struck The Founder's Father in the temple, knocking him over.

As The Founder's Father attempted to sit up, Mister Lewis closed the distance between them and stomped his foot on the sorcerer's forehead. The Founder's Father lay still.

Turning, he found the last two corpses on the ground. They twitched but were no longer moving with any purpose.

"I've got your man," Mister Lewis shouted to the sky. "You want to collect him?"

The last two corpses sprang back to their feet.

"We had every confidence you could resolve this situation," spoke the first corpse.

9. Dead Men Tell No Lies

The slap woke The Founder's Father up. He blinked twice and the image of two animated corpses leaning over him came into focus.

"Answer us," screamed the first corpse, throwing another backhand.

"You were bound to find me sooner or later," The Founder's Father struggled up to a sitting position. "I made my peace with the possibility. It would be preferable to see what happens next with my own eyes, but you're too late to stop it."

"Explain that," the first corpse repeated the backhand.

"You'll find out in good time," The Founder's Father wiped the blood off the corner of his mouth and paused to lick it off his hand. Then he glared at The Investor. "That avatar of avarice ruined my world. I'm returning the favor. I wouldn't want to live past the first wave, anyway."

The two corpses turned to stare at The Investor, who was hyperventilating.

"It's about his child," said Mister Lewis. "All of this is about his child stealing his grimoires and putting them online."

"Where are your spellbooks?" the first corpse screamed at The Founder's Father. "If you cannot secure them, we will."

"It doesn't matter where they are," came the reply. "My child walks the Earth once more and these unappreciative fools will reap what they sowed."

"Hey," stammered The Investor, pointing towards the entrance to the house. "Where did The Founder's body go to?"

"Explain," hissed the second corpse. "We disposed of the child. The body was eaten. The brain devoured. There was not enough left for you to reanimate."

"He was working on the body when we got here," interjected Mister Lewis. "It was in a chair over there. Looked like he was trying to patch it up."

The Founder's Father laughed.

The second corpse closed its eyes in concentration for a moment before speaking.

"Nothing was reanimated here, save for what was lying in this yard. Nothing remains animated that he controlled."

"And yet my child got up and walked away," cackled The Founder's Father. "You're supposed to be great guardians of necromantic knowledge. How could I ever do something beyond you?"

"Enough games," the first corpse grabbed the Founder's Father by the throat and didn't stop squeezing while life was still there.

"Yes," said the second corpse. "The living may lie to us, but the dead cannot."

The two corpses raised their arms and chanted in a long-forgotten language. The Founder's Father opened empty eyes and slowly, awkwardly stood up.

"Where are your spellbooks?" asked the first corpse.

"Destroyed," The Founder's Father's corpse spoke in a monotone. "They served their purpose and were no longer needed."

"Where is your child?" asked the second corpse.

"My child walks the Earth again."

"A misdirection," the first corpse tilted a puzzled head. "You resist from beyond the veil? Truly, you are a wonder. A direct answer to a direct question, servant: where is your child?"

"Inner," stammered The Founder's Father's corpse. "Inner pocket."

"Fetch it," growled the first corpse.

The Founder's Father's corpse moved a stiff arm to reach into his coat... and missed.

"Very well," hissed the first corpse. "We'll get it for you."

The first corpse lumbered over and ripped the coat open with one motion. There was an audible clink, a flash of white light and then both the first corpse and Founder's Father's corpse erupted into flames.

"I guess he did figure on getting caught," said Mister Lewis. "Looks like some kind of incendiary grenade rigged to go off. He really didn't want to be interrogated."

"The spellbooks are destroyed," said the second corpse. "The rogue actor is destroyed. It does not appear whatever he did with his child was necromancy. If the child does walk the Earth, it is outside our remit, so it is between your client and the child."

"And if it turns out to be some kind of necromancy you're not familiar with?" asked Mister Lewis.

"We are... how do your people say... around?"

The second corpse fell to the ground.

"That seems a little... brusque," said The Investor.

"Hey, we're talking about people who'd kill a guy and reanimate him just to save some time questioning him. These are not nice people. It just happens that our interests have been aligned for a time, but they weren't wrong about wanting to police their own. In most other situations, we wouldn't be cooperating with them. Might not happen again."

"But if The Founder isn't a zombie, what's going on?"

"I don't know. That guy was casting some weird spells the whole time and necromancy isn't the only form of magic. It could be anything. Of course, that doesn't mean the Necromancers were right about that."

"Was it a bluff?" asked The Investor.

"You don't set up a contingency plan to cremate yourself if you're bluffing. There's some plan in motion and he went to extreme lengths to keep it a surprise. What it is... we may not know until it's on us."

The two stood silent for a moment. Flames crackled over what was left of the corpses and creeped towards the house.

"We should probably leave before the fire spreads," said Mister Lewis. "The world will be better off if this place cleanses itself."

The Altar of Avarice

1. Don't Call It a Comeback

The sky was the wrong color. There was a tinge of red to it. While the smoke from massive fires could cause the sky to look that way, nothing was ablaze. Mister Lewis thought it a bit too much of a coincidence for the sky to change colors after a sorcerer had been making threats of doom and ruin.

He shrugged and returned to his phone. It was the fifth time he'd seen an ad for a video called "The Celestial Return." It turned out the advertising people weren't joking when they said that repetition was the key to engagement. Curiosity got the better of him and he clicked.

A man with flames where his eyes should have been appeared on the screen. When he spoke, there were more flames inside his mouth.

"We shall burn with prosperity," screamed the burning man. "The flames will bring you what you desire, even as it consumes your enemies."

Mister Lewis wasn't entirely sure if this was a movie trailer, or a televangelist had spent some money on special effects. The message was certainly familiar.

"Gorgul wants you to succeed," screamed the burning man. "And Gorgul wants his cut."

Mister Lewis almost dropped his phone. He scrolled down and saw that the video had 12,384,139 views.

The skies were correct. A storm was coming.

2. Money Doesn't Burn on Trees

"I'm glad you're here," cried The Investor. "I'm being embezzled."

"That can wait," said Mister Lewis. "We may have a bigger problem."

"Not having money to pay you is a pretty big problem," The Investor was coming unhinged. "Somebody is using my funds to advertise a video about... burning things for prosperity."

"The Gorgul video?"

"Yes, I think there's a Gorgul mentioned in it. And somebody's burning my money to promote it. And it's worse than that. The video is on Vidtrist. I own Vidtrist outright. And they've somehow replaced all the paid ads on the platform with in-house ads for that damn video. I have no revenue now."

The Investor picked up a keyboard and drew back an arm to throw it before thinking about replacement costs and stopping.

"And yet," sighed Mister Lewis, "Your video platform has probably never been so popular."

"I suppose if you want to look at it that way," The Investor muttered. "We are having some strain on the servers."

"Gorgul burns your money but brings you prosperity. That's how it's said to work. Consumes your sacrifice and takes a piece of the action of what comes next. I thought you shut down all of your holdings so something like this couldn't happen?"

"I did shut down all my apps," said The Investor. "Besides, nobody knows I own Vidtrist. It's buried beneath two shell corporations. It's a moneymaker for me. You can't expect me to go without cash flow."

"It's almost poetic," Mister Lewis shook his head sadly. "A god of greed getting reintroduced to the world on a platform that's only online because you couldn't live for a week without money. I hadn't given The Founder's Father enough style points."

"Wait," stammered The Investor. "That's what this is?"

"I'd better walk through this slowly," said Mister Lewis. "Gorgul is a god of greed. No, you haven't heard of him and that's kind of the point. His worship was stamped out in the early Bronze Age by the Hittites, 3000, maybe 3500 years ago. Nasty piece of work, that one. Sort of an arsonist running a protection racket. That was one of his anointed priests in the video. The fire where the eyes are supposed to be? Probably not special effects. Give Gorgul tithings or he burns you down. The tithing gets split up with his most favored followers, so it's kind of a proto-pyramid scheme, too."

"This Gorgul is the Avatar of Avarice he was talking about?" asked The Investor.

"No, he probably thinks you're an avatar. This is him returning the favor for his child. Let me distill it for you: The Founder's Father raises a god from the dead by getting it some new followers. Step one is probably just getting his name out there so it exists again and can be recognized. That'll cause the spirit to stir. I suspect that isn't the first video..."

"It wasn't," interrupted The Investor. "It's the third. It's more popular by far, but it looks like this has been going on for a week."

"Right, you get his name being said enough, the spirit stirs and there's enough power there to anoint a priest. That thing that looks like it's going viral? That's step two: if it gets popular enough, if it converts believers, Gorgul could manifest."

"I don't see what this has to do with me," The Investor sniffed.

"That must take effort," muttered Mister Lewis. "You noticed how the sky was the wrong color today? Approaching the color it gets when there are massive forest fires? That's how close he is to manifesting. The main question is whether the plan is to have Gorgul burn your businesses to the ground or if you've been earmarked as a blood sacrifice and whatever creature The Founder has been turned into intends to personally slit your throat. Given the parental instigation of all this, I'd bet on the latter.

"Now where is this company of yours and where are the servers with these videos on it?"

"The office is in the basement," The Investor was uncharacteristically quiet. "A server farm is attached to it."

"Then let's go downstairs and pull the plug," Mister Lewis was half out the office door. "Do buildings this old normally have spaces suitable for a server farm in the basement?"

"There are ways to get construction permits," said The Investor as they moved towards the stairwell. "If you're disciplined about keeping labor costs down, it's not that bad to configure. Cheaper than a new building."

Mister Lewis was struggling to suppress a comment about getting what you pay for when someone emerged from the stairwell. Someone with flames where their eyes should have been.

3. Fanning the Flames

The shadow cast by the hoodie made the flaming eyes stand out a little more than they might otherwise have. The anointed priest hissed, and the crackling of a fireplace could be heard beneath the hiss.

"There a bathroom around here?" asked Mister Lewis.

The Investor pointed down the hall.

"I'm going to test a disposal method from the legends," continued Mister Lewis. "If it doesn't work, run. An anointed priest isn't supposed to be human anymore."

"It's not a zombie?" asked The Investor.

"Go hold the bathroom door open," said Mister Lewis.

The Investor backed up towards the bathroom.

The priest took that as a cue and charged at The Investor.

Mister Lewis stepped aside and let the priest charge but grabbed its arm as it passed and put it in a full nelson.

"Does it want to kill me?" asked The Investor, pausing at the bathroom door.

"Sacrifice is probably the technical term," Mister Lewis lifted the priest off its feet, keeping the full nelson in place. "At least it isn't very strong."

The priest's feet flailed wildly as Mister Lewis walked it into the bathroom, chose a stall and shoved the priest's head in a toilet bowl.

"The legend says the only way to kill one of these is to extinguish the flame," explained Mister Lewis.

The priest thrashed around for a few seconds before going still.

Mister Lewis pulled the head out of the toilet and let the body hit the floor. The eyes sockets were empty and scorched, while a final wisp of smoke left the mouth.

The Investor leaned in for a better look and frowned.

"I think that's one of my employees," said The Investor. "Worked on applying database theory to human consciousness."

"The creepy data kid from the basement?" asked Mister Lewis, taking a second look at the face. "Explains why it wasn't stronger, I suppose. Hey, did this kid work next to that video server room?"

"That project is in the front of the basement," replied The Investor. "Vidtrist is in the back. It was convenient to store the databases next to the server farm, so we put them on the same level and just laid some fiber between the farm and that office."

"Not a good sign," Mister Lewis took a cautious step towards the door. "We better be quiet on our way down there."

The pair slunk back towards the stairs but were interrupted by shouting at the far end of the hall.

A new figure in a hoodie left one office and walked right into the one next to it. Two figures with flames for eyes followed four steps behind it.

Mister Lewis threw an arm over The Investor and flattened against the wall.

"The two in the rear," he whispered. "More employees?"

The Investor nodded.

"I proclaim you free," came a booming voice from the far end of the hall. "Awaken and give praise to your new master."

A crackling noise followed. Twenty seconds later, the figure in the hoodie emerged from the office. It stopped dead in its tracks and seemed to stare at The Investor.

"I've found you at last," the figure reached up and pulled back the hood, revealing the stitched together face of The Founder. The eye sockets were still empty from where the zombie ants had dined on The Founder's soft tissues and a set of runes shimmered on the forehead.

"Who the hell makes a golem with flesh?" muttered Mister Lewis.

Five figures with flaming eyes emerged from the office behind The Founder.

"There, my priests," The Founder pointed at The Investor. "Go and get Gorgul's tribute."

The priests stepped forward.

"Throw all your money at them, right now," Mister Lewis said to The Investor.

The Investor tossed three stacks of bills and the five priests dived on them like starving squirrels fighting over a nut.

"Run for the front door," said Mister Lewis, dragging The Investor by the arm.

"Not the financial tribute," The Founder howled in frustration as they ran.

4. Exit Strategies

"Tell me this is bulletproof glass," said Mister Lewis, slamming the front door as they fled the building.

"Of course," replied The Investor. "We wouldn't want thieves breaking in."

"Good," said Mister Lewis, shoving pennies into the doorframe above and below the door's handle. "The legends seem to be correct about the priests not being any stronger than their hosts and I don't see your crew breaking this down anytime soon."

"You called The Founder a golem?" asked The Investor.

"Think of it as... a magic version of a robot," replied Mister Lewis. "They're usually made out of clay, not body parts. It's not important right now. If that thing is just walking around your offices converting priests, this whole thing is a lot further along than I expected."

"Vidtrist is designed to go viral," said The Investor. "That just means our design works."

A priest hit the door. It didn't budge, but Mister Lewis and The Investor took a step back anyway.

"Anyway," continued Mister Lewis, gazing up. "See how the sky is getting redder? That means we're close to Gorgul manifesting. Right now, that thing occupying what's left of The Founder's body needs to be in close proximity to the victims in order to anoint priests. Gorgul manifests, that'll start happening from a distance and it'll be impossible to contain."

Two more priests were now pounding on the front door.

"Is it turning my staff into these fire eyed things to get at my money?" asked The Investor.

"You should take about five paces to your right," said Mister Lewis as he stepped back in the opposite direction.

The Investor stepped to the side. There were now eight priests inside the door and their gaze followed The Investor's path.

"That's what I thought," said Mister Lewis. "They have eyes only for you. Probably under some kind of compulsion and if you're the tribute, you're probably earmarked as a blood sacrifice. Kill you for personal revenge and then you're what unleashes Gorgul. We're dealing with a seriously nihilistic vendetta here. The compulsion is something we can work with in the near term, but I'm probably going to need to destroy those servers.

"Can't you just kill The Founder?" asked The Investor. "Make it all stop?"

"I can't kill something that isn't alive," said Mister Lewis. "Even if I destroy... whatever it is... there's still a building full of anointed priests and videos floating around. Gorgul will eventually manifest. It might be better if I blow up the entire building."

"You can't do that," The Investor actually jumped.

"Why not?"

"Those servers are the backups for all my companies, and it sounds like I don't have any staff left."

Mister Lewis glanced back at the door. It was up to twelve priests trying to get out.

"Against something like that, the only chance your staff would have of surviving would be to be out of the building at lunch when The Founder came knocking on their office door. Don't you back up to the cloud?"

"Of course, I back up to the cloud," screamed The Investor. "I built my own cloud and it's in the sub-basement."

"And that's the only place you have backups? Everything would be lost? With that data kid dead, there'd be no more mind swapping?"

"Especially the human consciousness data project! There's no one qualified to recreate it!"

Mister Lewis paused to exhale.

"Then I guess I won't be billing you for today," Mister Lewis shrugged.

"I forbid you to touch my property," The Investor took two steps forward with eyes suddenly filled with violence but thought better of it.

"Let's get something straight," growled Mister Lewis. "If I make it through this, you're still going to be alive and Gorgul isn't going to be barbequing half the county and seizing assets from the other half. We are both going to take one for the team."

"Can't you just call those Necromancers?" pleaded The Investor.

"Nothing in there is undead," said Mister Lewis. "And there's no time to go looking for them. Let me put this to you in business terms. If Gorgul manifests on this plane, there's going to be a massive body count. You'll be lucky if only half your customers die and that's before you figure in potential customers who will no longer be among the living. It's bad for revenue. It's bad for growth. It's bad for business in pretty much every measurable way. Would you concede that preventing Gorgul from manifesting is therefore good for business?"

The Investor finally shut up.

5. The Custodial Cleanse

Twenty priests were now trying to open the door, the combined glare from the fire that replaced their eyes reflecting off the glass in disturbing patterns.

"Back up to the edge of the parking lot," Mister Lewis said to The Investor. "But whatever you do, stay in a straight line with the door. If they can see you, they'll try to get at you and that'll keep them out of my hair. If they break free, get in the Hummer and don't stop driving until the sky is blue again."

The Investor backed up. Mister Lewis walked around the building and entered through the side door. Sure enough, while he could hear a loud and growing commotion around the front door, the hallway where he'd entered was empty.

Halfway down the hall, he heard heavy footsteps in the stairwell. A stream of anointed priests started pouring into the hallway and running towards the front door. Mister Lewis was standing in front of a door marked "janitor" and ducked in until things quieted down, three minutes later. As he opened the door to leave, he noticed a box of spray cans containing industrial degreaser. He stuck two cans in his coat pockets and took a third one in his hand.

The commotion by the front door seemed to be continuing, so he assumed the pennies were still holding the door in place. He paused at the stairs. No sound was coming from either direction, so he headed down.

The basement level seemed quiet. Mister Lewis first stuck his head in the Data Guru's office. It seemed undisturbed. They probably had no idea what was going on when The Founder showed up to anoint them into the priesthood. He took a closer look at the walls. Unfinished wood propping up rough cut support beams. A quick and dirty retrofitting, but the haste in which it was put up might prove useful in a worst-case scenario like this.

He returned to the hall and noticed another janitor's closet across from the door marked "Vidtrist." He peeked in to find a bounty of cleaning solutions. Smiling, he closed the door.

The Vidtrist office had a little better furniture than some of the other offices in The Investor's portfolio. Perhaps cash flow made them a favored child or perhaps whoever worked here invested some of their own money to pretty up an unfinished workspace. The office went deep, the length of the building from that point.

For some reason, the four desks in the room had been pushed together, forming a sort of large table. Computers, monitors and assorted office supplies lay scattered on the floor around the desks, like someone had run an arm across the desks to clear them. Two of the monitors were broken.

It was only the first 15 feet or so of the room that was office space. The remainder of the room was taken up by servers and the familiar hum of fans filled the room.

Along the wall was a fuse box. He opened it, consulted the chart and flipped a switch that should have shut off a quarter of the servers. An overhead light went off at the back of the room, but the servers appeared to still be running.

Puzzled, he flipped the next four switches. The lights over the rest of the servers went out. Not only did the servers appear to still be running, the servers were glowing.

Mister Lewis approached the closest server rack. The servers were definitely running. He reached behind it, located the power cord and pulled it out. The servers were still running.

He lifted the can of degreaser and sprayed the middle server on the rack. Nothing happened.

"Very clever," came a booming voice from behind. "But how can the accelerant spark and ignite if there is no electricity?"

Mister Lewis turned to see The Founder, forehead runes and all, standing in the doorway to the office.

"Servers run hot. Heat can ignite a degreaser just as easy as electricity."

"But those machines are powered by my prayers," laughed The Founder. "And my prayers run cold."

"Then you won't mind if I spray a few more," Mister Lewis turned back to the servers and sprayed up and down server racks on each side of the aisle.

"Why don't you come here, and I'll show you Gorgul's altar?" said The Founder.

"Oh, is that what that is?" Mister Lewis stepped deeper into the server farm. "If I understand your quest properly, my blood on that altar isn't what will usher Gorgul's physical presence into this world."

"Truly a clever one," mused The Founder. "But Gorgul is closer to this world than you think. The videos are a success. I have anointed many priests. The sacrifice of the defiler's servant would now suffice to open the gate. You are... good enough."

"You are the most talkative golem I've ever met," called Mister Lewis from the back of the room. "Is that part of being made from flesh? Or whatever flesh was left? I know your brain was eaten at the same time your eyes were."

"Golem is such a reductionist term," said The Founder. "My father made me to be many things. Evangelist to Gorgul. Sword of vengeance. Guide to this corrupt society's well-earned reward."

"It really is fascinating that you have so much personality." Mister Lewis discarded the empty degreaser can and pulled a fresh one from his pocket. "Did your father put a new brain in your skull? Is something else in there? You've got me curious."

"Come here and perhaps I'll show you," replied The Founder.

"I'm a little busy here," Mister Lewis moved to the back corner of the room, spraying the nearest rack with degreaser. "You wouldn't happen to have a match on you?"

The Founder said nothing but marched down the row of servers. When it got to the end, it swung a fist at Mister Lewis. A wide hook thrown a little too wide. It caught the last server rack in the row and sent it skidding.

The rack sparked when it hit the floor and ignited the degreaser.

"Thanks for the light," said Mister Lewis.

The Founder swung again. Mister Lewis sidestepped and The Founder buried its fist in the support post he'd been standing in front of. As The Founder tried to free its fist, Mister Lewis sprayed its face with the degreaser can, coating its face and covering the runes on its forehead.

The Founder staggered. The runes on its forehead were still pulsating, but they were starting to drip. Mister Lewis dragged his sleeve across the runes. The runes wiped off and The Founder fell limp.

"Definitely a golem," muttered Mister Lewis to the body. "Let's see what got into your head."

There were stitches on the top of The Founder's head, but as he reached for them, the servers that were still upright began to shake. He turned to find an image starting to form above the server farm. The image of a head that was not altogether human.

"You're way ahead of schedule," as Mister Lewis sprinted for the janitor's closet, a string of expletives crossed his lips.

A bottle of carpet cleaner was tossed around the server racks that hadn't been sprayed. A jug of ammonia was set next to a support post towards the front of the room. A can of degreaser was stuck in the hole The Founder's fist had made in the support beam at the back of the room.

It was then that he noticed the image above the server farm open its eyes.

Mister Lewis ran back to the janitor's closet, grabbed an armful of random cleaning supplies and tossed them in the general direction of the server farm. He returned to the closet and emerged shoving a length of aluminum foil into a large bottle of drain cleaner. He sealed the cap and threw the bottle to the back of the room, landing next to The Founder's body and the smoldering server that had fallen over.

He ran out of the room and towards the stairs. When he got to the top of the stairs, the commotion was thankfully still audible at the front door as he bolted for the side exit.

6. Customer Satisfaction

"Start walking that way," Mister Lewis gestured to The Investor as he emerged from the building.

The Investor started walking as Mister Lewis ran over.

"You never got around to installing sprinklers in the basement?" asked Mister Lewis.

"No," said The Investor. "And why am I walking over here?"

"Because the priests will try to follow, and I'd like them over the server farm just in case it works."

"In case what works?" asked The Investor.

"I tossed a bottle bomb before I left," explained Mister Lewis. "In a couple minutes, that bottle's going to blow and release a small cloud of hydrogen gas that'll get ignited by a burning server and that explosion should ignite a bunch of cleaning supplies. Worst case scenario, it ought to burn up those servers. Maybe with a minor amount of shrapnel."

A boom came from the building.

"Was that your bomb?" asked The Investor.

"That was the first part," said Mister Lewis. "Now we see if gravity cooperates."

The Investor shot him a confused look but said nothing.

"Let's back up out of the parking lot," said Mister Lewis.

Smoke started seeping out of the building as they backed up.

"When you remodeled the basement for that server farm, did you take out some load bearing walls?" asked Mister Lewis.

"Yes," said The Investor. "They put in some support posts. Expensive."

It was then that the building collapsed on itself.

"Probably less supports than you should've had, and it looks like what you had must've been damaged in the explosion and fire," said Mister Lewis pulling The Investor further back. "You should stay away from there for a while. I threw a lot of cleaning supplies towards where the fire was going to be, and I didn't really have a chance to check every last one. You know what happens when you mix that stuff... could be some noxious fumes or worse."

"Does fire insurance pay against arson?" The Investor had a blank expression.

"It does if it wasn't you setting the fire," replied Mister Lewis. "So, let's get your story straight. You're now going to go get something to eat. That's why you weren't in the building. Early lunch. Make sure people see you."

"Those things with the fire eyes, you said they couldn't be killed."

"A building collapsed on them and there's a fire at the bottom eating up all the oxygen. No oxygen, no fire, no more anointed priests. Depending on how much fire is burning down there, the coroner might be a little confused by what he finds, but won't be conclusive.

Strange burn patterns on people who were supposed to be in the building."

"The entire staff turned into those... things?"

"Yeah," said Mister Lewis. "That thing made from The Founder's remains was already upstairs before either of us knew what was going on. If they came to work, they stopped being human at least 15 minutes ago."

"Then there's a silver lining."

"Since when did you start looking on the bright side?"

"Its terrible publicity when you fire people," The Investor cracked a thin smile. "And if I can locate any offsite backups, a lot of equity just failed to vest. I can start over with more shares than I had in the first place."

Mister Lewis stared at his client, shook his head and muttered "some people never learn," as he walked away.